I0648241

J. Boulvin

The Entropy Diagram

and its applications

J. Boulvin

The Entropy Diagram
and its applications

ISBN/EAN: 9783337406233

Printed in Europe, USA, Canada, Australia, Japan

Cover: Foto ©Andreas Hilbeck / pixelio.de

More available books at **www.hansebooks.com**

THE

ENTROPY DIAGRAM

AND ITS APPLICATIONS

BY

J. BOULVIN

PROFESSOR AT THE UNIVERSITY OF GAND, BELGIUM

TRANSLATED FROM THE 'REVUE DE MÉCANIQUE' BY

BRYAN DONKIN

M. INST. C.E.; M.I. MECH. E.; M. AMER. SOC. M.E. ;
M. INST. GERM. E.

WITH THIRTY-EIGHT FIGURES

London:
E. & F. N. SPON, LTD., 125 STRAND

New York:
SPON & CHAMBERLAIN, 12 CORTLANDT STREET

1898

PREFACE

BY THE TRANSLATOR.

———◦◊◦———

This work first appeared in French in 1897, as a series of articles in the
'Revue de Mécanique,' a new and excellent technical journal published
at Paris. They attracted the notice of the translator, who considered
that they were well worth translating. At his request the Author
consented to put them into book form, and by kind permission of the
publishers of the Revue, MM. Dunod of Paris, they are now given in
English to the public. Professor Boulvin is not only a well-known
writer of various technical books, but also a theoretical and practical
engineer of many years' standing. He was among the first to popu-
larise the use of the entropy diagram as an accurate means of teaching
thermodynamics, and his work is the more valuable, because there are
at present very few treatises on the subject. It may be considered as
a short syllabus of the principles of thermodynamics as applied to heat
engines, and its chief claim to originality lies in the systematic method
of using temperature and entropy diagrams. M. Boulvin published a
more elaborate treatise in French, in 1893,* in which the entropy
diagram and its application to the solution of thermal problems was
described, and its relation to the ordinary pressure and volume diagram
demonstrated for the first time with mathematical precision. He also
furnished the materials for a short article on the same subject, which
appeared in 'Engineering,' January 1, 1896.

There is one difficulty in the use of the new entropy diagram. Pro-
perly speaking, it ought only to be applied to reversible cycles, such as
are supposed in theory to take place in the cylinders of heat engines.
Entropy in its strict sense has no meaning if employed to represent the
changes of state of a fluid flowing through a vessel, and more or less

* 'Cours de Mécanique appliquée aux Machines,' 3ᵉ vol., Paris (E. Bernard).

throttled in its passage, like the admission and exhaust steam in a steam engine cylinder. Some authors who have not given this fact sufficient attention, have drawn deductions from the diagram of heat which cannot be verified, or have even mistaken the interpretation of the phenomena it is intended to illustrate.

A little consideration, however, will enable us to avoid these errors. The Author has succeeded in an extremely simple and elegant way in deducing the heat balance from the entropy diagram of a steam engine by a graphic method, instead of Hirn's process of heat analysis, which is long, requires intricate calculations, and gives the results under a numerical form only. To show this heat balance graphically, the only way has hitherto been to plot diagrams in which the quantities of heat were converted into equivalent areas representing work, superposed on the indicator diagram, and to the same scale. But these diagrams were incomplete. They showed only the exchanges of heat between the steam and the walls, and not the more important item of the total heat expended and lost during the cycle, or per stroke, nor the dryness fraction of the steam, and the superheating which may occasionally take place during compression and expansion. For all gases, and especially for steam, a certain simple relation exists between the Temperatures, Pressures, Volumes and Entropy. From these the Author has designed a graphic diagram of convenient shape and size, by means of which a complete heat balance of an engine test can be obtained, and the movements of heat during any part of the stroke followed at a glance. Nothing has to be calculated except the simple proportions required to determine the scale. This is a most important and practical result.

The best standard method of calculating the Heat Efficiency of a steam engine has been much discussed, and the question would be practically solved if, for every steam engine, we had entropy diagrams traced to the same scales of temperature and entropy for a unit weight of steam coming from the boiler. These diagrams could be compared with each other in any country, and the smallest variations in the work of each engine graphically shown, without any explanation being necessary.

For this English translation, Professor Boulvin has added a new method of dealing with the clearance steam and throttling during admission, by means of which the wall action may be ascertained and represented graphically during the separate periods of the indicator diagram, irrespective of compression, whether complete or not.

Metric weights and measures and degrees Centigrade have been, of necessity, used throughout this translation, on account of the French figures and diagrams.

Prof. Unwin, F.R.S., has kindly read over the English proofs, and our best thanks are due to him for his valuable suggestions.

As the subject of Entropy is still in its infancy, and no complete works on it have yet appeared, the following list of references to it, with the names of authors and dates of publication, may be found useful by students and others. References are placed, as far as possible, in order of date of publication.

BIBLIOGRAPHY OF ENTROPY.

BELPAIRE, TH. Bulletin de l'Académie Royale de Belgique. 1872. (See note p. 2.)

GIBBS, J. WILLARD. Graphical Methods in the Thermodynamics of Fluids. Transactions of the Connecticut Academy of Arts and Sciences, U.S. April 1873.

LINDE, PROF. Theorie der Kälteerzeugungsmaschine. Munich, 1875.

SCHRÖTER, PROF. Ueber die Anwendung von Regeneratoren bei Heissluft-maschinen. Zeitschrift des Vereines deutscher Ingenieure. Berlin, 1883.

HERMANN. Die graphische Behandlung der mechanischen Wärmetheorie. Berlin, 1884.

ZEUNER, G. Technische Thermodynamik. 3rd edition, Leipzig, 1887-90.

GRAY, MACFARLANE. The Rationalisation of Regnault's Experiments on Steam. Proceedings Institution of Mechanical Engineers, London, 1889; Institution of Civil Engineers, vol. cxiv.

COTTERILL, PROF. The Steam Engine considered as a Thermodynamic Machine. London, Spon, 1895.

RICHMOND, G. Refrigeration Process in Thermal Dynamics. Transactions of American Society of Mechanical Engineers, vol. xiv. 1893.

WILLANS, P. W. Steam Engine Trials. Minutes of Proceedings of Institution of Civil Engineers, London, vol. xcvi. 1888-9; vol. cxiv. 1892-3, part iv.

BOULVIN, PROF. J. Cours de Mécanique appliquée aux Machines, vol. iii Théorie des Machines Thermiques. Paris, E. Bernard, 1893.

MOLLIER, R. Das Wärmediagramm. Berlin, 1893.

SANKEY, CAPT. Proceedings Institution of Civil Engineers, London, vol. cxiv. (see Willans); vol. cxxv. 1895–6. Proceedings of Institution of Mechanical Engineers, February 1894 (see Professor Beare's paper on Marine Engine Trials), five entropy curves of marine engines.

EWING, PROF. J. A. The Steam Engine and other Heat Engines. Cambridge, 1894.

BOULVIN, J. Entropy and Entropy Diagrams, translated by Bryan Donkin. Engineering, January 3, 1896.

RIPPER, PROF. W. Superheated Steam Engine Trials. Minutes of Proceedings of Institution of Civil Engineers, London, vol. cxxviii. 1896–97, part ii.

REEVES —. The Entropy-Temperature Analysis of Steam Engine Efficiencies. Sydney, 1897.

ANCONA, UGO. Das Wärmediagramm der gesättigten Dämpfe und seine Anwendung auf Heiss- und Kaltdampfmaschinen. Zeitschrift des Vereines deutscher Ingenieure, Berlin, April 1897.

KRAUSS, FRITZ. Graphische Kalorimetrie der Dampfmaschinen. Berlin, 1897.

GOLDING, HENRY A. The Theta-phi Diagram. Several articles in the 'Practical Engineer,' London, 1898.

CONTENTS.

CHAPTER VI.

STEAM ENGINES.

b

APPENDIX.

ILLUSTRATIONS.

———◆◇◆———

THE ENTROPY DIAGRAM

AND

ITS APPLICATIONS.

—◦—

INTRODUCTION.

AN Entropy Diagram is a graphic representation of the successive thermal changes in a body, produced by the simultaneous variations of two of the co-ordinates characterising its condition—namely, Temperature and Entropy. The meaning of Temperature is too well known to detain us now, and we propose to define it accurately later on. Entropy, however, does not correspond to any external attribute of a body, although it belongs to it in the same way as its internal energy, pressure, or volume. To make the subject clear to those who are not familiar with the study of thermodynamics, it will be necessary briefly to recapitulate the fundamental principles of that science. Our explanation shall, however, be as short as possible, because the chief object of this work is to set forth the advantages offered by the Entropy Diagram in solving thermal problems. We propose to illustrate the theory by numerical examples, and to give all necessary information regarding the choice of scales, units of measurement, etc.

We have had occasion to observe how abstract theories of thermo-dynamics, which are slowly grasped, and often considered useless and misleading by practical men, become attractive and clear when graphic-ally treated and combined with an Entropy Diagram. For instance, what a laborious task it would be to reason upon the external work done by a fluid, at varying pressures and volumes, without the help of the graphic method of representation devised by Watt, brought into general use by Clapeyron, and now so well known through indicator diagrams. If we had been unacquainted with this invention until now, how useful it would be to illustrate the action of a steam engine. The Entropy Diagram shows in the same way the movements of heat, and entropy

curves hold to heat problems the same position that indicator curves do
to mechanical energy.

Although Entropy and Temperature were used as co-ordinates more
than twenty years ago by Gibbs and Linde,* they were little known
until brought forward in the papers and discussions of the Institutions
of Mechanical Engineers and Civil Engineers (London), by Macfarlane
Gray and Willans. Since then this method has rapidly become popular,
both in teaching and for research; and if the theories with which it
deals seem at first a little difficult and abstruse, the persevering reader
will soon convince himself that they can be applied practically. By
presenting the subject in a condensed and handy form, we hope to
show that it is capable of solving problems of daily occurrence.

CHAPTER I.

FUNDAMENTAL LAWS OF THERMODYNAMICS.

I. THE study of the changes produced in bodies by heat is based upon
certain *fundamental laws*, as the laws of Mariotte (or Boyle), and of Gay-
Lussac (or Charles). There are also certain well known experimental
facts, such as that the specific heat of all permanent gases is a constant,
Regnault's data relating to steam, etc. To all bodies, however, two
fundamental principles are applicable, expressing two kinds of relations
in which their temperatures, volumes, pressures and other properties
stand to each other.

The first of these laws is known as the Mechanical Equivalent of
Heat. The second is called Carnot's Principle, although the views of
this great physicist were inaccurately expressed by him, and had to be
corrected by Clausius after the discovery of Joule's Equivalent.

Carnot's cycle comprises a series of operations succeeding each other
in the following order: (1) Communication of heat to the body, and its
expansion at constant temperature, or isothermal expansion; (2) Expansion without gain or loss of heat, or adiabatic expansion; (3)
Compression with abstraction of heat, the temperature being maintained

---

* They were first mentioned by Th. Belpaire in the 'Bulletin de l'Académie royale
de Belgique,' 1872, vol. 34, but in an abbreviated form. The author did not make any
practical use of the idea.

constant, or isothermal compression; (4) Adiabatic compression of the body, and return to its initial condition.

This is called a reversible cycle, because it can be carried out in the inverse direction by simply changing the sequence of operations. But to effect it, the body must during the cycle be at the same temperature as the source of heat or cold, and at a pressure equal to the external pressure upon it. If these conditions are realised, an extremely small difference of temperature or pressure will determine the direction in which the transformations of heat and work take place. Carnot's principle can only be applied to reversible cycles, while the law of the Mechanical Equivalent is of general application, and holds good for irreversible operations, such as the flow of steam or gas under a head of pressure.

II. *Carnot's Principle.*—For all bodies with which the Carnot reversible cycle is carried out between two limits of temperature, the ratio between the heat turned into work during the cycle, and that imparted from the source of heat, does not depend upon the nature of the body, but only upon the temperatures of the sources of heat and cold. This ratio is :

$$\frac{Q_1 - Q_2}{Q_1} = \frac{T_1 - T_2}{T_1} ;$$

Q_1 being the heat abstracted from the source of heat; Q_2 the heat given up to the source of cold. T_1 and T_2 are the respective temperatures of the sources of heat and cold, as shown by an air thermometer, the zero of which is 273° C. below the ordinary zero, and they are called "absolute" temperatures.

The above ratio is the thermal efficiency of the cycle, and shows the quantity of heat it is able to turn into work, in proportion to that supplied from the source of heat. To demonstrate Carnot's principle we must apply Clausius' postulate, namely, that heat cannot of itself pass from one body to another at a higher temperature. This proposition means that heat can only be communicated from one body at a higher to another at a lower temperature, and the excess of temperature necessary for the transfer of heat may be produced either by chemical combination or by mechanical energy. If this were not so, the great masses on the surface of the earth, water, mountains, and the surrounding air, might be utilised gratuitously as sources of heat in prime motors, to replace coal and other fuels.

Starting from this experimental axiom, it is easy to prove that two heat engines carrying out the Carnot cycle within the same limits of temperature will have the same thermal efficiency. If they had not, one of them with the same quantity of heat would do more work than the other. Suppose the two engines were so mechanically connected that the cycle in the weaker were reversed, that is, that work in it were converted into heat, it would be drawn round by the larger engine, and work would be produced without a corresponding expenditure of heat. The smaller engine would thus refund to the source all the heat withdrawn from it by the larger motor. The result would be to produce work for nothing, which is impossible.

Since the efficiency of any Carnot cycle between the limits T_1 and T_2 of absolute temperature is the same for all fluids, it must be a function of the temperature—of what nature remains to be seen. This function can be determined from the known properties of permanent gases.

Let us assume that a unit weight of one of these gases undergoes the successive transformations of a Carnot cycle, while abstracting Q_1 thermal units from the source of heat, and yielding Q_2 thermal units to the source of cold. From the law of heat equivalence and the properties of gases we have the equation

(1)
$$\frac{Q_1}{Q_2} = \frac{T_1}{T_2},$$

or

$$\frac{Q_1 - Q_2}{Q_1} = \frac{T_1 - T_2}{T_1},$$

a ratio which, according to **Carnot's principle**, is the same for **all** bodies.

III. *Analytical deductions from Carnot's principle.*—The last equation may also be written as follows:

$$\frac{Q_1}{T_1} - \frac{Q_2}{T_2} = 0,$$

or

(2) .
$$\Sigma \frac{dQ}{T} = 0.$$

The symbol Σ means that if each **separate** quotient $\frac{dQ}{T}$ for the changes which **the fluid** undergoes in the four periods of a Carnot cycle be added together, the result is **zero**. Adiabatic operations have no effect upon the total, because in **them**

$$dQ = 0.$$

Equation (2) can be applied to the curves of a group of Carnot cycles (Fig. 1). If each be expressed by a similar equation, and all are added together, the total will be composed only of the quotients $\frac{dQ}{T}$ of the portions *a b*, *c d*, *e f*, *g h*, etc., of the curves, which cancel each other, and therefore the result will be zero.

Equation (2) is also valid for any closed cycle (see Fig. 2). Let us integrate for this cycle the differential quotient as follows:

$$\int \frac{d\,Q}{T},$$

d Q being the heat supplied along the element *a b*, Fig. 2, and T the absolute temperature at, say, point *a*. If the adiabatics *a a′*, *b b′*, be

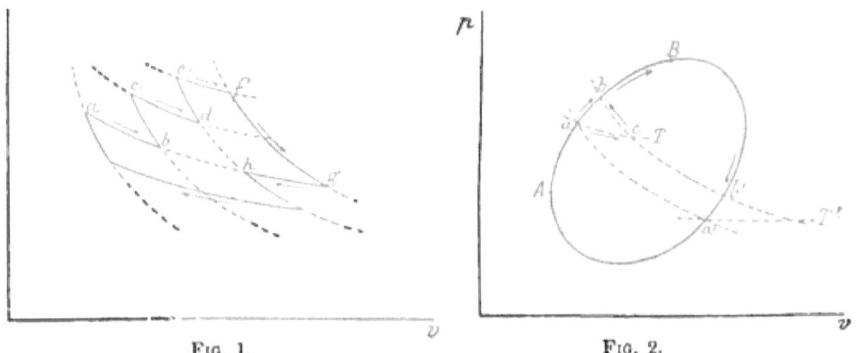

Fig. 1.   Fig. 2.

drawn through points *a* and *b*, and the isothermals T and T′ at *a* and *a′*, the whole cycle may be thus subdivided into small Carnot cycles like the one in Fig. 2. We obtained for these cycles the following equation:

$$(3) \qquad \Sigma \frac{\Delta\,Q}{T} = 0.$$

Here Δ Q is the heat supplied along the line *a c*, or for the operations *a c*, *c b*, the latter line being part of an adiabatic.

But the quantity of heat supplied along the lines *a c*, *c b*, differs from *d* Q (heat supplied along *a b*) only by the quantity of heat corresponding to the extremely small area of work represented by the triangle *a c b*. Thus we may substitute *d* Q for Δ Q in the integral, and we have for any closed cycle

$$\int \frac{d\,Q}{T} = 0.$$

We have now proved that if for any given cycle the different quotients are added together, the total will be composed of positive and negative elements cancelling each other, that is to say, if these differential quotients be added or subtracted along a straight line according to their positive or negative value, the sum will be equal to zero, or in other words, the initial point will coincide with the point of departure. But instead of completing the cycle, if we take only a portion A B of the curve (Fig. 2), the sum will have a value depending on the law of the application of heat to the body, and its temperature during the operation. Hence, there is a function S, which for points A and B, has the values S_A and S_B, and we have

$$S_B - S_A = \int_A^B \frac{d\,Q}{T}.$$

To this function S Clausius gave the name " *Entropy* "; $d\,S$ or $\frac{d\,Q}{T}$ is its differential, which is positive or negative with $d\,Q$, while T, the absolute temperature, is always positive; $S_B - S_A$ is the change of entropy when the body passes from condition **A** to condition B.

CHAPTER II.

TEMPERATURE-ENTROPY, or T S (θ ϕ) DIAGRAM.[*]

IV. LET us suppose the relation between **T** and **S** to be known, and let us draw the values of T as ordinates, and the corresponding values of

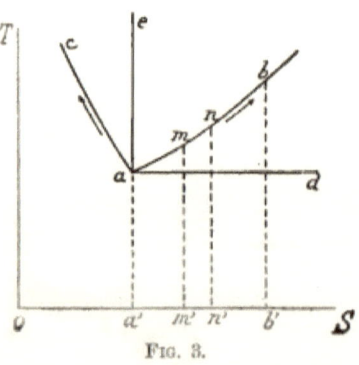

FIG. 3.

S as abscissæ (Fig. 3). As the entropy at the starting point is arbitrary, we will take any length $o\,a'$ for the value S_A. If the line be continued from a' to b', to represent $S_B - S_A$, it will give the increase of entropy along A B in the $p\,v$ diagram Fig. 2, $a\,b$ being the corresponding curve in a T S diagram. This curve $a\,b$, representing the relation between T and S, may always be determined, for, if the changes in pressure and volume of a unit weight of any body be known, the change of temperature can be deducted from them, and also the change in internal energy and work

---

[*] The symbols generally used in England for Temperature and Entropy are θ and ϕ, and the diagram is known as the Theta-phi diagram. The letters T and S have been retained in this translation, to utilise the original French drawings.

done. The application of heat dQ is equivalent for each element to the change in internal energy, plus the work done. Thus the change in entropy dS or $\dfrac{dQ}{T}$ may be calculated, and to each point on the pv line corresponds a point m on the T S diagram.

The elementary area of this diagram is

$$m\,m' \times m'\,n', \quad \text{or} \quad T\frac{dQ}{T}, \quad \text{or} \quad dQ,$$

or

Temperature $\times$ entropy = thermal units supplied.

In the curve ab (Fig. 3) dQ is a positive quantity, as entropy is increasing, but for the line ac, dQ would be negative, and heat would be abstracted. There are certain special operations which are easy to represent. Thus, whatever the nature of the fluid, the isothermal line ad, Fig. 3, is parallel to S, the adiabatic ae for which dS is zero (that is, there is no change of entropy) is parallel to the ordinate T. From these general conclusions the following deductions may be drawn, which should assist in defining the relations between temperature-entropy and pressure-volume lines.

1. *If the pressure-volume (p v) diagram is a closed cycle, the entropy diagram will also be closed,* because in both the total increase of either temperature or entropy is *nil,* and therefore the final values of both will be the same as the original values. In this case the area of the T S curve represents the heat supplied in the same way as the area of the pv diagram represents work done.

2. *The Carnot cycle in the new system of co-ordinates is a rectangle, Fig. 4.* The heat turned into work is

$$Q_1 - Q_2 = (S'' - S')(T_1 - T_2).$$

The heat supplied is

$$Q_1 = (S'' - S')\,T_1.$$

The thermal efficiency of the cycle is the ratio of the two, or

$$\frac{Q_1 - Q_2}{Q_1} = \frac{T_1 - T_2}{T_1}.$$

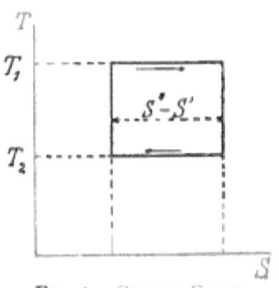

FIG. 4.—CARNOT CYCLE.

If the increase of entropy is the same, the heat supplied to effect an isothermal operation is in proportion to the absolute temperature. The latter should be regarded as a definite quantity, similar for example to a definite weight of water falling from a certain height.

3. *If two curves intersect each other in a pv diagram, the same will happen in the corresponding entropy diagram.* In both (see Fig. 5) there are two points, A B and a b, which are common to the two curves A M B and A N B in the p v diagram, and a m b and a n b in the entropy diagram.

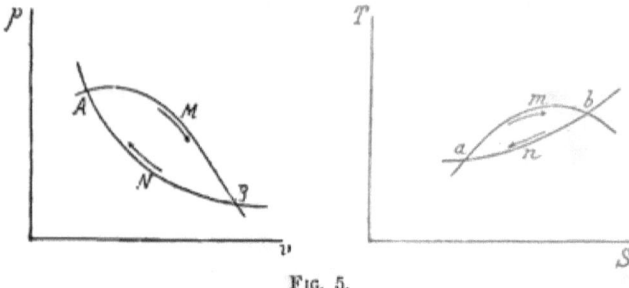

FIG. 5.

The two curves a m b, a n b cannot coincide throughout unless A M B, A N B also form one line. For if we imagine A M B N A to form a closed cycle, producing a definite quantity of work, a m b n a will represent an equivalent quantity of heat supplied, and therefore a m b and a n b must enclose a definite area.

4. *If two p v curves are tangential, the corresponding T S curves will also be tangential.* For if the distance between the two points A B, Fig. 5, is gradually diminished, the same will be the case with a b, and in both systems the two curves will have a common element.

5. In the *entropy diagram, the isothermal and adiabatic lines always intersect each other,* because they are parallel to the co-ordinates, hence we may conclude that *they will also cut each other in the p v system.*

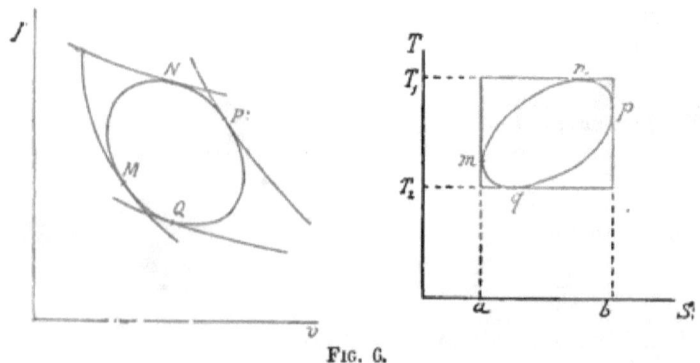

FIG. 6.

6. *In the p v diagram any closed cycle can be drawn within the lines of the Carnot cycle,* and will **touch** it at the points M N P Q, Fig. 6. If

the same cycle be drawn in T S co-ordinates, it will fall within the rectangle representing the Carnot cycle, and come in contact with it at the points $m\,n\,p\,q$.

V. *Cycles of maximum efficiency.*—Such a cycle is formed by the Carnot, no other imaginable cycle converting more heat into work between the same limits of temperature. For in the closed curve $m\,n\,p\,q$ (Fig. 6) the heat turned into work is $m\,n\,p\,q$, while the heat supplied is $a\,m\,n\,p\,b$; the thermal efficiency is the ratio between these two quantities. We get from the above figures

$$\frac{m\,n\,p\,q}{a\,m\,n\,p\,b} \; < \; \frac{T_1 - T_2}{T_1},$$

and thus

$$\rho \; < \; \frac{T_1 - T_2}{T_1}.$$

VI. There are, however, a number of other cycles having the same efficiency as the Carnot within the same range of temperature, and it is with these we now propose to deal.

In the entropy cycle (Fig. 7), let $a\,b\,c\,d$ be formed of the isothermal lines $a\,b$ and $c\,d$, and of the two lines $b\,c$ and $d\,a$. The line $b\,c$ is arbitrary, but $d\,a$ is drawn parallel to it. Thus the heat turned into work during the cycle is $a\,b\,c\,d$, or the equivalent rectangle $a\,b\,m\,n$, but the heat supplied from the source of heat is $d\,d'\,a\,a' + a'\,a\,b\,b'$; that is to say, it is greater than the heat required to carry out the same work in a Carnot cycle. Now the heat given up to the source of cold consists of two parts, $c\,d\,d'\,c'$, which passes to the cold

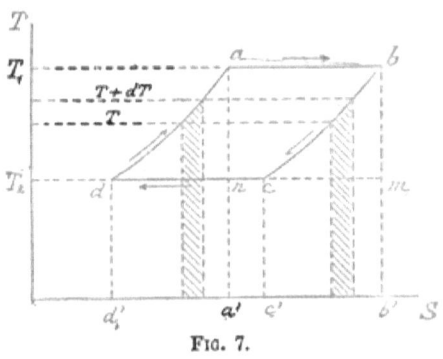

Fig. 7.

source at the lowest temperature T_2, and is wholly lost, and $b\,b'\,c\,c'$, which is strictly equal to the heat required to carry out the operation $d\,a$. Instead of being wasted this heat might be held in reserve, and communicated to the fluid along $d\,a$, thus producing work without the intervention of the source of heat. Thus the adiabatic lines of the Carnot cycle would be replaced by the two lines $b\,c$, $d\,a$, which compensate each other, and the efficiency of such a cycle, formed of two isothermals and of two of these lines called "isodiabatic," by Rankine, would be equal to that of the Carnot cycle. We will now consider in what way the lines *b c, d a* may be said to compensate each other.

Heat does not flow spontaneously from one body to another at a higher temperature. Thus the heat given up along *b c* can only be refunded, and utilised to effect the operation *d a*, if the process be subdivided into very small differences of temperature. The heat given up along *b c* between the temperatures $T + d\,T$ and T, and represented by the shaded area on the right, might be stored, and supplied along a portion of *d a*, as shown by the shaded area on the left. The difficulty is to find a practical method of storage, or regenerator. We may assume that it will offer large heat-conducting surfaces, and consist of a number of subdivisions at all temperatures between T_1 and T_2. To accomplish the operation along *b c*, the working fluid passes successively through these divisions, and deposits in each a part of its heat. To refund this heat along *d a* without a fresh supply, the fluid must pass again through the divisions in the reverse direction, from the coldest to the hottest. This ideal process can only be roughly and approximately realised, because the regenerator has a limited conductibility, and can only store up heat if the fluid is at a much higher temperature, and refund it if the working agent is much colder. Therefore only the upper portion of the line *b c* can be utilised to refund heat gratuitously along the lower part of *d a*.

Thus the Carnot cycle should have a higher efficiency in practice, because it can work without the addition of a regenerator; other points, however, should also be taken into consideration.

CHAPTER III.

APPLICATION OF THE ENTROPY DIAGRAM TO PERMANENT GASES.

VII. Let us take an operation represented in the *p v* diagram by the equation

(1)
$$f(p, v) = 0.$$

For a permanent gas Boyle's and Gay-Lussac's laws give

(2)
$$p\,v = R\,T,$$

R being a constant for all gases, equal to $a\,p_o\,v_o$; a is the coefficient of expansion $= \frac{1}{273}$, p_o the standard atmospheric pressure; v_o specific volume of the gas at pressure p_0 and temperature 0° C. (32° F.). For permanent gases the specific heats C at constant pressure and c at constant volume are constants for each gas, and proportional to v_0, that is in inverse ratio to the specific weight. The ratio $\dfrac{C}{c}$, which is designated by γ, is a constant for all gases, and its value is about 1·4.

For calculation the following Table will be found useful:

TABLE OF PROPERTIES OF GASES.

——	$\dfrac{1}{v_0}$ *	R	C	c	Remarks
Atmospheric air	1·293187	29·272	0·23741	0·16838	* $\dfrac{1}{v_0}$ is the weight of the gas at 0° C. (32°F.) at standard atmospheric pressure, 10,334 kilos. per sq. metre (14·7 lbs. per sq. inch).
Oxygen . . .	1·429802	26·475	0·21751	0·15426	
Hydrogen . .	0·089578	422·612	3·409	2·41773	
Nitrogen. . .	1·256157	30·434	0·2438	0·17291	
Carbonic oxide .	1·250511	30·283	0·245	0·17376	† Carbonic acid diverges more or less from the other gases.
Carbonic acid † .	1·9774	19·154	0·202	0·157	

The equation deduced from the law of the Mechanical Equivalent of heat is

$$d Q = c \, d T + A \, p \, d v,$$

$c \, d T$ being the heat absorbed to increase the temperature, $A \, p \, d v$ the heat equivalent to the external work done.* The above equation, supplemented by equation (2), gives

(3) $$d S = \frac{d Q}{T} = c \frac{d T}{T} + A R \frac{d v}{v}.$$

The heat absorbed to raise the temperature of $d T$ at constant pressure is $C \, d T$, while that required to raise the temperature at constant volume is $c \, d T$; the difference $(C - c) \, d T$, is equal to the amount necessary to effect expansion at constant pressure, namely

$$(C - c) \, d T = A \, p \frac{d v}{d T} \, d T,$$

or if combined with equation (2)

$$C - c = A R.$$

Equation (3) may be thus written

(4) $$d S = c \frac{d T}{T} + (C - c) \frac{d v}{v}.$$

* The symbol A is used as the reciprocal of the Mechanical Equivalent.

To trace the T S diagram corresponding to equation (1) of the $p\,v$ diagram, the entropy must be calculated as a function of the temperature, by eliminating v from equation (4).

VIII. *Study of the operations corresponding to equation* $p\,v^k = p_1\,v_1{}^k$; k being a constant, $p_1\,v_1$ co-ordinates for a given point. Equation (1) is replaced by

(1¹) $p\,v^k = p_1\,v_1{}^k$,

and we may write

(2) $p\,v = R\,T$ (4) $d\,S = c\,\dfrac{d\,T}{T} + (C - c)\dfrac{d\,v}{v}.$

Dividing equation (1¹) by (2) we get

$$R\,T\,v^{k-1} = p_1\,v_1{}^k.$$

Calculating from it the value of $\dfrac{d\,v}{v}$, and substituting it in equation (4), we get

$$d\,S = c\,\frac{k-\gamma}{k-1}\,\frac{d\,T}{T},$$

or by integrating between the limits T_1 and T, for which the entropies are S_1 and S,

(A) $S - S_1 = c\,\dfrac{k-\gamma}{k-1}\,\log_e\dfrac{T}{T_1}.$

This equation may be applied to any transformation expressed in the $p\,v$ system by equation (1¹), whatever the value of k. Nearly all compression and expansion curves obtained from the indicator diagrams of air and gas engines, etc., follow equation (1¹). They differ only in the value of k, which can be calculated from the co-ordinates $p_1\,v_1$ and $p_2\,v_2$, when these are known for two points of the curves, because $p_2\,v_2{}^k = p_1\,v_1{}^k$; or taking their logarithms

$$k = \frac{\log p_1 - \log p_2}{\log v_1 - \log v_2}.$$

The values of $p_1\,v_1$ and $p_2\,v_2$ may be calculated from an indicator diagram without the help of the scales of pressures and volumes, if the exact area of the clearance space, which does not appear in the diagram, is accurately known, but the least error in its dimensions may greatly influence the value of k. This, in the Author's opinion, is the reason why this exponent differs so greatly in the compression curves of gas engines.

Equations (1¹) and (A) practically include all variations in the expansion or compression of permanent gases. For isothermal lines, as T is a constant, equation (2) gives

$$p\,v = \text{constant},$$

which is identical with (1') if k is made equal to unity; thus

$$k = 1 \text{ for isothermal lines.}$$

For adiabatic lines, S being a constant, equation (A) gives

$$k = \gamma.$$

For values of k differing from γ, heat must be either supplied or abstracted. The following table gives the particulars of the curves for different values of k.

TABLE OF TRANSFORMATIONS, $p\,v^k = p_1\,v_1{}^k$ (Figs. 8 and 9).

Number of Curve, Figs. 8 and 9.	$p\,v$ Co-ordinates.		T S Co-ordinates.	
	Value of k.	Form of the Curve.	Value of $c\,\dfrac{k-\gamma}{k-1}$.	Form of the Curve.
1	0	p = constant	c	}S and T increase or
2	$0 < k < 1$	$p\,v^k$ = constant	$> c$	} decrease together.
3	1	{ $p\,v$ = constant or common hyperbola }	∞	T constant.
4	$1 < k < \gamma$	$p\,v^k$ = constant	negative	{ S increasing, T decreasing, or *vice versâ*.
5	$k = \gamma$	{ $p\,v^\gamma$ = constant or adiabatic }	0	S = constant.
6	$\gamma < k < \infty$	$p\,v^k$ = constant	$< c$	}S and T increase or
7	∞ *	v = constant.	c	} decrease together.

* Sign of infinity.

Curves 1 and 7, Figs. 8 and 9, might be found without calculation, for if the pressure is constant we get

$$d\,S = \frac{d\,Q}{T} = C\,\frac{d\,T}{T},$$

or by integration

$$S - S_1 = C \log_\epsilon \frac{T}{T_1},$$

and for constant volume

$$\frac{d\,Q}{T} = c\,\frac{d\,T}{T},$$

or by integrating

$$S - S_1 = c \log_\epsilon \frac{T}{T_1}.$$

Figs. 8 and 9 show the connection between the $p\,v$ and the entropy diagrams. All the curves start from the same points A and a. The full lines mark the increase of entropy in both diagrams, the dotted lines the diminution of entropy; or, in other words, the addition or subtraction of heat in the direction of the arrows. In the T S diagram, as may be seen from equation (A), the increase of entropy when passing

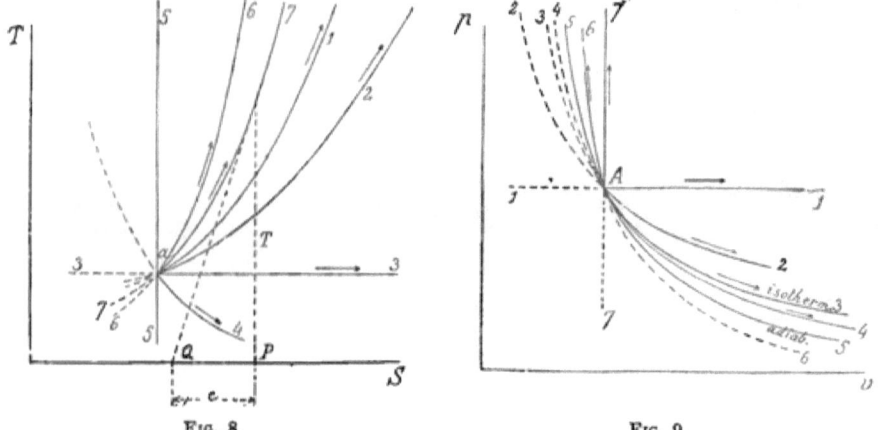

FIG. 8.   FIG. 9.

from T_1 to T is proportional to a constant, the value of which depends upon k only, and upon the hyperbolic logarithm of the ratio of the absolute temperatures. When k has the same value, there is no change in the entropy line; thus the curves in which $p\,v^k = $ constant, are all isodiabatic for the same value given to k: that is, they afford cycles of maximum efficiency when combined with two isothermals.

Curves of constant pressure and of constant volume have been much used in air engines, in combination with two adiabatics or two isothermals, to avoid the cumbrous cylinder required to carry out the Carnot cycle.[*]

[*] See the Author's 'Théorie des Machines Thermiques,' Paris, Bernard, 1893, where hot air and refrigerating engines are fully treated.

IX. The curves represented by equation (A) are of such a nature that in each of them it is necessary that the supply of heat be proportional to the increase of temperature. Thus, in operations at constant volume we get

$$d\,S = c\,\frac{d\,T}{T},$$

or

$$c = T\,\frac{d\,S}{d\,T};$$

that is to say, the specific heat at constant volume is represented by the subtangent P Q of the entropy curve (Fig. 8), the length of which is the same for any point on the curve. The same holds good for constant pressure lines, where the subtangent is C. Moreover, for any value of k we have

$$c\,\frac{k - \gamma}{k - 1} = T\,\frac{d\,S}{d\,T} = \frac{d\,Q}{d\,T}.$$

Thus the coefficient $c\,\dfrac{k - \gamma}{k - 1}$ is the specific heat corresponding to $p\,v^k = $ constant.

Hence we may conclude that for any curve the subtangent is a constant, and represents the particular specific heat belonging to the process under consideration. Besides the ordinary specific heats c and C, which govern lines of equal volume or equal pressure, there are an infinite number of other constant specific heats, differing according to the value of k in $p\,v^k = $ constant. If a gas be adiabatically compressed, it passes from a low to a high temperature without any addition of heat, which makes the specific heat equal to zero; if it be isothermally expanded, the heat supplied is infinite in proportion to the variations of temperature, which are nil : in this case the specific heat is infinite.

CHAPTER IV.

APPLICATION OF THE ENTROPY DIAGRAM TO GAS ENGINES.

Beginning with the theoretical treatment of our subject, we propose first to deal with the working conditions of the well known *Beau de Rochas* or *Otto cycle* gas engine, and compare it with that of an original Lenoir non-compressing engine. We will then draw the Entropy diagram of such a motor, basing it on data supplied by an actual trial, and discuss the results, and finally we will calculate the heat balance, and show the way in which the total heat developed has been employed.

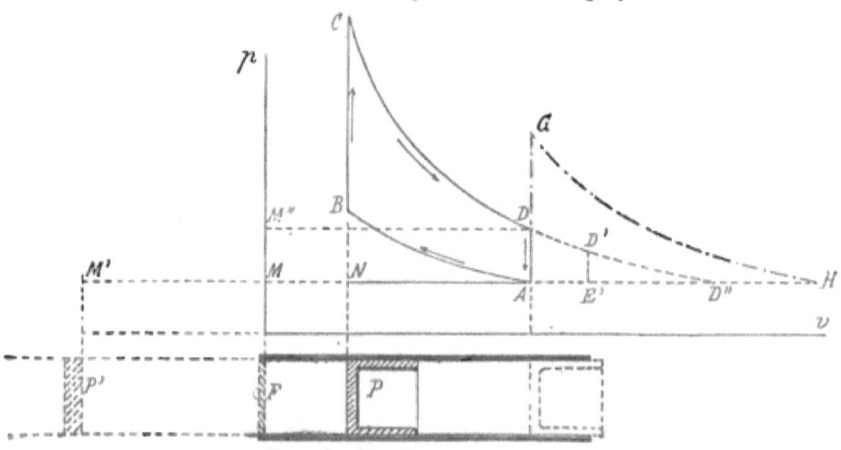

Fig. 10.—Gas Engines Diagrams.

X. The successive operations carried out in the cylinder of an Otto engine (see Fig. 10) are :—

1. N A, Drawing in the charge ; the piston stopping at point A, the volume of the charge is M N (clearance or compression chamber) + N A. The mixture in the cylinder consists of the fresh charge, plus the burnt products in the clearance space.

2. A B, Compression of the mixture, which is first assumed to be adiabatic.

3. B C, Increase at constant volume of the pressure developed by the explosion of the charge, the combustion being supposed instantaneous and complete.

4. C D, Expansion of the burnt gases, also assumed to be adiabatic.

5. D A, A N, Exhaust. D A marks an instantaneous fall in pressure, produced by the opening of the exhaust valve; A N is the line of discharge at constant pressure, which is nearly atmospheric pressure.

In this engine the cycle is not closed, and only operations 2, 3 and 4 are carried out wholly in the cylinder. Our task will be to assimilate the above diagram (Fig. 10) to that of a closed reversible cycle.

Let us suppose that the explosion chamber, instead of being cast in one with the cylinder, is replaced by a movable partition F, and the cylinder lengthened towards the left, where it is furnished with an auxiliary piston P'. The fresh charge of gas and air is assumed to be shut in between P' and F, its volume M' M being equal to N A. During operation 1 (admission) both pistons P' and P move simultaneously to the right, the action of piston P' merely replacing the effect of the pressure of the atmosphere. Having reached position F, auxiliary piston P' remains stationary during operations 2, 3 and 4, and forms the back of the explosion chamber. At point D on the diagram, piston P' is released and moves to the left, producing the same sudden drop in pressure from D to A as if the exhaust valve were opened. It is even projected to the left beyond its original point, while the working piston P remains at point A. The burnt gases enclosed between the two pistons are cooled to their original temperature, and their volume will be approximately the same as that of the charge before compression M A,* which will complete the cycle.

To begin a new cycle, the volume M A of burnt gases is replaced by a fresh charge at the same volume, pressure and temperature. This substitution causes no change in the cycle, as it can be effected without expenditure of energy or heat.

As far as the thermal changes taking place in a gas engine, and work done are concerned, the action may be described as follows, taking A as the starting point: A B, adiabatic compression of the mixture enclosed in the cylinder and clearance space; B C, C D, communication of heat to the mixture at constant volume, and adiabatic expansion; D A, cooling at constant volume. If adiabatic expansion were continued to D', cooling at constant volume would take place from D' to E' with a fall to atmospheric pressure, and a return to the initial temperature along the

---

* We say approximately, because a certain amount of condensation is produced by combustion, and thus the volume of the burnt gases is less than that of the fresh charge before explosion at the same temperature and pressure. But the contraction is small, because a portion of the burnt products do not vary in composition, or contract, and there is a large proportion of inert N. We are thus led to conclude that although combustion is internal, the mixture may be treated as an inert gas, to which heat is communicated from without.

line E' to N; if it were carried to D" and the pressure fell to atmosphere, there would finally be a subtraction of heat at constant pressure. In all types of Otto engines, expansion cannot be carried beyond point D, because the cycle consists of four strokes of equal length. In the Atkinson engine, now no longer made, expansion was continued beyond this point, and the expansion stroke lengthened by an ingenious kinematic device.

XI. As we are now able to substitute *a closed cycle* for the actual sequence of operations taking place in a *gas engine*, it may be represented by its corresponding diagram of entropy and temperature co-ordinates (Fig. 11). Here A is the initial point at which the temperature is that of the mixture before compression; the entropy for this point being arbitrary, we may assume it to be zero. A B is the adiabatic compression, B C the explosion curve, along which heat is imparted at constant volume, represented by the equation (see paragraph VIII)

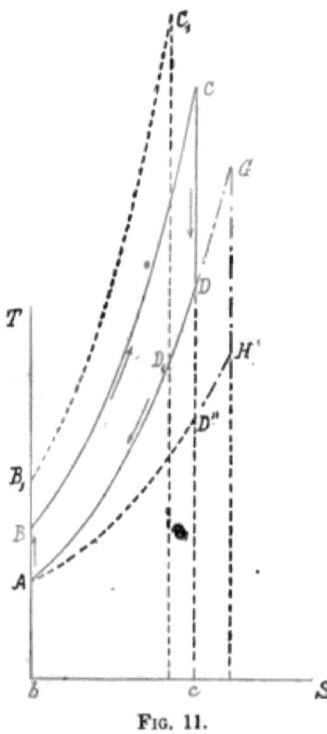

FIG. 11.

$$S = c \log_e \frac{T}{T_B}.$$

The heat developed by combustion is shown by the area $b\,B\,C\,c$, C D is the adiabatic expansion of the charge, and the cycle is completed by the curve D A at constant volume, showing the return of the fluid to its initial condition, and expressed by the equation

$$S = c \log \frac{T}{T_A}.$$

Clearly, a relation must exist between A D and B C, since for the same values of S, the temperatures are in a constant ratio. The heat turned into work is shown by the area A B C D, the heat lost is shown by A D c b. If expansion were complete to atmospheric pressure, the adiabatic line C D would be continued to D", and we should have D" A as the line of constant pressure.

XII. The effect of *initial compression* is to improve the efficiency. If we imagine an engine in which the clearance space or combustion chamber were gradually reduced in size, the total weight of the charge, including the burnt products, being the same, we get the diagram A B₁ C₁ D₁, Fig. 11. Here the heat evolved by the explosion is the same, but the loss of heat to the refrigerator is less, and therefore more work is done with the same weight of gas. It is easy to calculate the increase in pressure and in the maximum temperature of explosion produced by increased compression of the charge. The effect of incomplete expansion is shown by the loss of the area of heat in the triangle A D D″; this loss is diminished when initial compression is increased. With less initial compression, the distance between point B and point A is reduced. For a non-compressing engine with the same weight of the charge, same quantity of gas, and complete expansion, the *p v* diagram will be A G H, Fig. 10, and the T S diagram A G H, Fig. 11, showing that the loss of heat is much greater than in compression engines. As the temperature developed by explosion is the same, the area enclosed by the curves B₁ C₁, B C, A G, are equal, and H being to the right of D″ in the T S diagram, shows that the temperature is higher. If we assume expansion to be complete in both cases, the non-compressing engine, although the pressure of explosion in it is much lower, will require a larger cylinder than the compression engine.

XIII. *Application of the Entropy Diagram to an Otto Gas Engine.*—For this purpose an experiment has been selected made by Professor D. S. Capper, in January 1895, on a 7 horse-power nominal Crossley-Otto gas engine, in which all the data were determined, and results tabulated, with great care.[*] A chemical analysis was made, both of the gas for the charge and of the burnt products, and the heat carried off by the cooling jacket water estimated.

Cylinder Dimensions and Results of the Trial.

Diameter of piston, 215·9 millimetres = 8½ inches.
Length of stroke, 457·2 ,, = 18 ,,
Volume of explosion chamber, 6·985 litres = 0·246683 cubic feet.
Duration of experiment, 40 minutes.
Revolutions per minute (mean), 172·1.
Number of explosions per minute, 84·7.

I.H.P. { English, 12·8 } . B.H.P. { English, 11·47 } .
       { French, 12·97 }   { French, 11·62 }

Calorific value of the gas { per cubic metre, 5,438 cals. }
                           { per kilogramme, 10,500 ,, }

---

* See 'Gas, Oil and Air Engines,' by Bryan Donkin, page 421. Only the necessary figures are here reproduced. The charge was fired by hot tube, but the slight irregularities caused by the missed explosions, which were very few, are not taken into account.

Gas per hour (gas for the ignition not included),

$$\text{Per B.H.P.} \begin{cases} \text{English, } 741\cdot85 \text{ litres} \\ \text{French } 732 \quad \text{,,} \end{cases}.$$

Composition of the charge by weight,

Weight of gas in one explosion	. .	0 kil. 00087
Weight of air ,, ,,	. .	0 kil. 01517
Weight of burnt gases per charge	. .	0 kil. 00689
Total weight of mixture .	. .	0 kil. 02293
Heat generated by complete combustion of the charge (calculated)	. .	9·135 cals.

Composition of the charge by volume,

$$\frac{\text{Air}}{\text{Gas}} = 7\cdot27.$$

$$\frac{\text{Air} + \text{clearance products}}{\text{Gas}} = 10\cdot72.$$

Temperature of the charge before compression, 32·5° C.

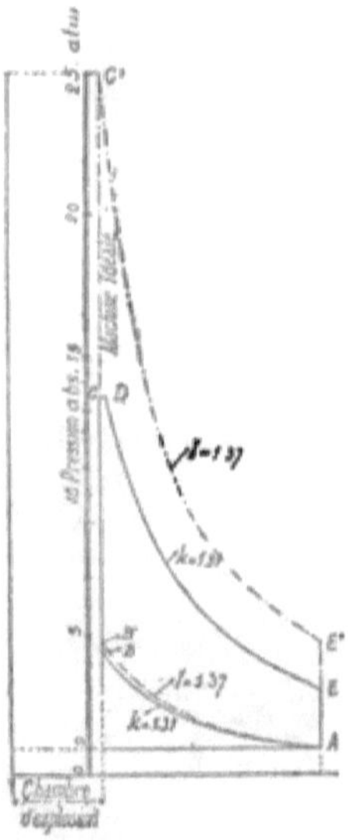

FIG. 12.—GAS ENGINE
INDICATED DIAGRAM.

The volume of the gas was measured, and its weight thus determined. The volume of the exhaust products was taken to be that of the clearance chamber, and their weight thus calculated, making the necessary corrections for pressure and temperature at the end of exhaust. The volume and weight of air were determined by difference, on the assumption that the temperature of the mixture at the end of admission was a mean between that of the surrounding air and of the jacket water. This is the mean temperature given above.

Nine indicator diagrams were taken during the experiment, which when combined give an average diagram represented by the full lines in Fig. 12. From this diagram the values of the exponent for both the compression and expansion curves have been calculated, the result being the equation $p\,v^{1\cdot31} = $ constant. The specific heats, c and C, of the mixture before ignition were calculated from its composition; the specific heats of the burnt products in the same way. Professor Capper gives the following values :

Before ignition $\begin{cases} c = 0\cdot1911 \\ C = 0\cdot2656 \\ \dfrac{C}{c} = 1\cdot39 \end{cases}$.   After combustion $\begin{cases} c = 0\cdot1931 \\ C = 0\cdot2656 \\ \dfrac{C}{c} = 1\cdot37 \end{cases}$.

Thus the calculated **ratio of the** specific heats differs from **the value** $1\cdot40$ **for** permanent gases, **because in some** of the chemical constituents of the **fresh gas, as carbonic acid, methane, and ethylene, the** ratio $\dfrac{C}{c}$ **is** smaller, **and the steam and** CO_2 **in the burnt products** also reduce its value. From a comparison **of the** specific **heats before and after ex-plosion, it would** appear that, **as** we have **already assumed, combustion does not practically affect the physical constants** c C, **nor** their ratio. **Therefore we need not take count of the chemical** changes during the **cycle, but may consider the mixture as a fluid** subjected to external heating **and cooling, and use the values of** c **and** C after combustion **for** the **whole cycle, making the exponent** γ **for** adiabatic **compression** or **expansion** $= 1\cdot37$.

The weight of the working fluid is $0\cdot002293$ kil., but we will trace the entropy diagram for a weight of one kilo. and afterwards modify the scale of the abscissæ, to adapt it to any weight. The absolute temperatures for points B C D E of the entropy diagram, Fig. 13, are calculated from the temperature before compression, at **point** A, which is assumed to be $273 + 32\cdot5°$ C. $= 305\cdot5°$ C. absolute. If we take p_a, v_a, T_a and p_b, v_b, T_b as the pressures, volumes and temperatures at points A **and** B respectively, we get

$$\frac{T_b}{T_a} = \frac{p_b\,v_b}{p_a\,v_a},$$

and the same applies to points C, D and E of the cycle.

The following values are calculated by this and other equations :

$$T_a = \quad 305\cdot5° \text{ C.}$$
$$T_b = \quad 443\cdot6° \text{ C.}$$
$$T_e = 1364\cdot4° \text{ C.}$$
$$T_d = 1460\cdot6° \text{ C.}$$
$$T_e = 1024\cdot4° \text{ C.}$$

For the entropy at these points we have

$$S_B - S_A = c \frac{k-\gamma}{k-1} \log_\epsilon \frac{T_b}{T_a}$$

$$S_C - S_B = c \log_\epsilon \frac{T_c}{T_b}$$

$$S_D - S_C = C \log_\epsilon \frac{T_d}{T_c}$$

$$S_E - S_D = c \frac{k-\gamma}{k-1} \log_\epsilon \frac{T_e}{T_d}$$

$$S_A - S_E = c \log_\epsilon \frac{T_a}{T_e}$$

$$c = 0 \cdot 1931$$
$$C = 0 \cdot 2656$$
$$\gamma = \frac{C}{c} = 1 \cdot 37$$
$$k = 1 \cdot 31$$

Hence we calculate

$$S_B - S_A = -0 \cdot 014$$
$$S_C - S_B = 0 \cdot 216$$
$$S_D - S_C = 0 \cdot 018$$
$$S_E - S_D = 0 \cdot 013$$
$$S_A - S_E = -0 \cdot 233$$

To construct the entropy diagram, Fig. 13, we have taken for the scale of the ordinates $\frac{1}{10}$ millimetre per degree of absolute temperature C., and for the abscissæ 500 millimetres per unit of entropy.* As already explained, this scale is only provisional, because the formulæ for calculating the entropy are for one kilo. of the fluid, while its weight throughout the cycle here considered was only $0 \cdot 02293$ kilo. Thus the scale must be multiplied in the same ratio, viz. $\frac{500 \times 1}{0 \cdot 002293} = 21805$ millimetres per unit of entropy. In the thermal diagram of the actual quantity of fluid used per stroke during the trial, a calorie is represented by a rectangle having 1° C. for its ordinate, and a unit of entropy for its abscissa, or according to the above scale an area of

$$0 \cdot 1 \times 21805 = 2188 \cdot 5 \text{ square millimetres.}$$

(See the shaded square in Fig. 13.) If the areas comprised within

---

* There is no name to denote the entropy unit, that is, the increase of the function $\int \frac{dQ}{T}$ for any body, where T calories are communicated to it at constant temperature T. This unit may also be taken as equal to the increase of entropy which corresponds to the evaporation at atmospheric pressure of 678 grammes of water.

To reproduce the diagram in the text the scales have been much reduced; the original drawing was three times as large.

the lines defining the cycle are measured **with a planimeter** according to
the scale indicated above, the **following results are obtained :**

I. Area A B *b a*, 0·1331 cal. **Heat absorbed by** the walls during
compression.

II. Area *b* B C D E *e*, 5·0629 **cals.** Heat shown in the diagram
during explosion, combustion at constant pressure, and
expansion. (**The course of** the line D E proves that **com-**
bustion continues **during** expansion.)

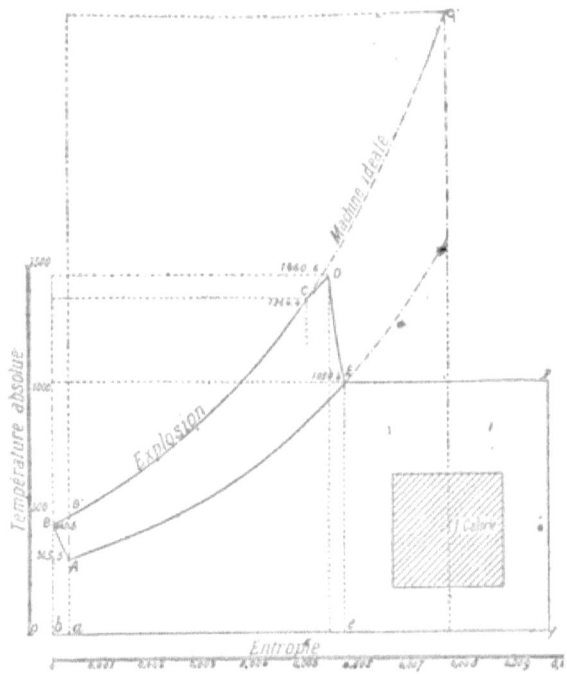

Fig. 13.—Entropy Diagram for an Actual Gas Engine Test.

III. Area *e* E A *a*, 3·148 **cals.** Heat lost by the exhaust gases.

IV. Area A B C D E, 1·7818 **cals.** Heat turned into work. According to Fig. 13, **we ought to have**

$$IV = II - (I + III).$$

This analysis only gives an account of the way in which the heat
developed by combustion and shown in the diagram by Area II or 5·0629

cals. has been employed. But the total heat evolved by complete combustion of the charge ought to have been 9·135 cals., and the difference or

$$9\cdot135 - 5\cdot0629 = 4\cdot0721 \text{ cals.,}$$

which have disappeared in some way or other, and are shown by the rectangle E F $f e$, Fig. 13.

We may now study the heat balance more closely. The internal surfaces of the cylinder and piston, Fig. 14, return after each cycle to their original thermal condition (or temperature); therefore the heat absorbed by the cast-iron surface of the inner wall A is equal to that lost from the external wall B. This loss is equal to the heat carried off by the jacket water, plus that lost by radiation from the piston and from the external surface of the barrel. We will call the heat lost to the jacket E, and that lost by external radiation R. The heat penetrating the cast-iron wall surface A consists of: (1) Heat absorbed by the wall during compression (surface I of the diagram = 0·1331 cals.); (2) An unknown quantity of heat x absorbed by the metal during explosion B C, combustion C D, and expansion D E, Fig. 13; (3) The heat y withdrawn by the metal from the hot gases during their fall in pressure E A and the exhaust to atmosphere. As the walls return to their initial condition after each cycle we have the following equation:

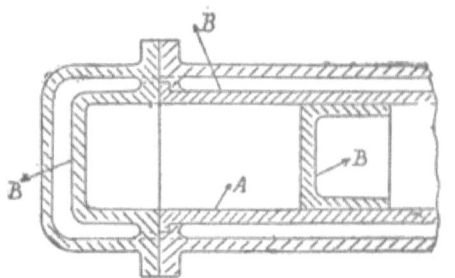

FIG. 14.—GAS ENGINE CYLINDER.

$$I + x + y = E + R.$$

Now, the heat x is the difference between the total heat of combustion, 9·135 cals., and the heat actually supplied during the cycle, which we found to be Area II or 5·062 cals., and is therefore equal to 4·0721 cals., represented by the rectangle E F $f e$.

By measuring the temperatures of the cooling water in and out, and its weight, experiments have shown that the value of E (heat lost to the jacket) for a complete cycle is

$$E = 4\cdot047 \text{ cals.}$$

The value of R has not been determined, but Prof. Capper assumes that it may be taken at 1·5 per cent. of the total heat generated. If we accept this figure we get

$$R = 0 \cdot 1370 \text{ cals.,}$$

and, according to the equation given above

$$y = E + R - (I + x) = -0 \cdot 0212 \text{ cals.}$$

y is therefore negative, that is to say, during the fall in pressure and the opening of the exhaust, the metal, instead of abstracting heat from the gases, imparts it to them, but the quantity is insignificant.[*]

The heat lost to the exhaust gases is Area III of the entropy diagram, or 3·148 cals., but to this must be added y, or the small quantity of heat the gases receive from the walls and carry off, namely 0·0212 cals. Therefore

$$3 \cdot 148 + 0 \cdot 0212 = 3 \cdot 1692 \text{ cals.}$$

represents the heat lost to the exhaust during the cycle.

We can now draw up the heat balance, showing the total expenditure of heat, as follows:

HEAT BALANCE.

—	Calories.	Per Cent.	Area in Diagram.
Heat generated by explosion	9·1350	100	b B C D E F f
„ turned into work	1·7818	19·50	A B C D E
Losses in detail :			
1. Heat absorbed by the walls during compression	0·1331	1·46	b B A a
2. Heat absorbed by the walls during the working stroke	4·0721	44·58	e E F f
Heat lost to the exhaust : Imparted by the gases to the Cals. atmosphere . . . . . 3·1692			
Taken up by the gases from the walls † . . . . . 0·0212			
3. Difference, or loss of internal heat by the gases . . . . 3·1480	3·1480	34·46	a A E e
Total loss of heat	7·3532	80·50	b B A E F f

---

† This heat refunded by the walls to the gases during exhaust forms part of the heat absorbed by the walls during the working stroke, and included under head 2. As it has already been accounted for, it must be deducted, as shown in the graphical heat balance in the last column.

---

[*] It is, however, possible that the gases may heat the metal walls at the moment after exhaust, and cool them afterwards. The value given above is the result of both these exchanges of heat.

If the heat losses be divided under the different heads of waste, they will work out as follows :

	Calories.	Per Cent.
Heat lost by the gases to the atmosphere	3·1692	34·70
„ to the jacket water	4·0470	44·30
„ by radiation	0·1370	1·50
Total loss	7·3532	80·50
Heat turned into work	1·7818	19·50
Cals.	9·1350	100·00

XIV. *Comparison of the Actual with an Ideal Gas Engine.*—In an ideal engine all the heat evolved by the complete combustion of the charge would be utilised to raise the temperature of the fluid at constant volume, compression and expansion would be adiabatic, and no heat lost to the walls. The entropy diagram of such an engine would be represented by the dotted lines in Fig. 13; A B′ would be the compression and B′ C′ the explosion line. The heat turned into work would be 3·3370 cals. or 37 per cent., the exhaust gases would carry off the remaining 63 per cent. of the total heat of combustion. The indicator or $p\,v$ diagram of such an engine is drawn in dotted lines, Fig. 12. The efficiency of the actual as compared with the ideal engine would be the ratio of heat turned into work in the two cycles, or

$$\frac{1\cdot7818}{3\cdot3370} \text{ calories} = 0\cdot54.$$

This trial is given only as showing the application of the entropy diagram to the results of an experiment, and not as illustrating the best results now obtainable in gas engine practice; but it affords a fair representation of an average test. In a similar calorimetric analysis of experiments made by Dr. A. B. Kennedy, and published by the Author, the compression and expansion curves differed from those here worked out, the values of the exponent being 1·38 for compression, and 1·43 for expansion. The calculated values of c and C were also higher, because the increase of these coefficients at higher temperatures, according to Mallard and Le Chatelier's laws, had been taken into account.

CHAPTER V.

STEAM AND OTHER GASES.

XV. The physical data available for the *study of gases* are obtained from Regnault's Tables, which give q, the heat necessary to raise the temperature of a liquid from 0° C. to any given temperature t, and r the latent heat of evaporation at different temperatures and the corresponding pressures. The sum of these two quantities $q + r$ is the total heat λ. Regnault has also calculated for all bodies their pressures as saturated gases at different temperatures.

With the exception of a few experiments on specific heat, little however is known of the properties of superheated steam. Regnault gives its specific heat at constant pressure as a constant, equal to 0·48, and this is about the same value as it would have if treated as a permanent gas, and its density calculated from its molecular weight. For all ordinary problems it will be sufficiently accurate to consider superheated steam as a permanent gas.

During evaporation at constant pressure the heat communicated to the liquid is employed to alter its state, and to do external work. The volume of the liquid u may be taken as a constant at all temperatures, because it expands very slightly with increase of heat, but the volume u' of a kilo. of the steam generated varies greatly at different temperatures, or at the corresponding pressures. The expansion produced by complete evaporation of the liquid is $u' - u$, and the heat equivalent to the external work done is

$$A\,p\,(u' - u).^*$$

Thus the total heat supplied to the body during its change of state from a liquid at 0° C. to its complete evaporation at constant pressure p, is made up as follows :

Total heat λ
$\begin{cases} q.\text{—Heat required to raise the temperature of the liquid} \\ \quad\text{from 0° to } t°\text{ C.} \\[1em] r.\text{—Heat of evaporation at constant temperature } t, \text{ or latent heat.} \begin{cases} A\,p\,(u'-u).\text{—Latent heat turned into external work.} \\[0.5em] r - A\,p\,(u'-u).\text{—Latent heat equivalent to increase of internal energy.} \end{cases} \end{cases}$

* For explanation of symbol A, see note, p. 11.

Evaporation may be incomplete, and all the liquid not completely converted into steam, in which case the condition of one kilo. of the mixture is characterised by its percentage of moisture x, denoting the dryness fraction of the steam. If, after complete evaporation has taken place, heat is still applied at constant pressure, the steam becomes super-heated. Thus the fluid may pass successively through the stages of superheated, dry saturated, and wet steam. For all kinds of liquids Regnault gives the following equations:

$$q = a\,t + b\,t^2 + c\,t^3$$
$$r = \mathrm{A} + \mathrm{B}\,t + \mathrm{C}\,t^2 + \mathrm{D}\,t^3,$$

the constants in which have been determined by him for all fluids used in thermal engines.

From the first of these equations we have

$$\frac{d\,q}{d\,t} = l = a + 2\,b\,t + 3\,c\,t^2,$$

l being the specific heat of the liquid, which varies with the temperature, but is nearly a constant for some fluids. For water a is = unity, and it must be so, as the specific heat of water at $0°$ C. has been taken as the standard, and when raised one degree C. forms one calorie, or French thermal unit. If t increases, l also increases slightly.

The increase in entropy of the fluid when heated from $0°$ C. to $t°$ C. is

$$s = \int_o^t \frac{l\,d\,t}{\mathrm{T}}.$$

It has been calculated for a complete scale of temperatures, for water by M. de Montchoisy, for various bodies by Zeuner, for CO_2 by Schröter, for SO_2 by Ledoux, etc. The increase of entropy during the process of evaporation is found by dividing r by the absolute temperature, which remains constant, as the operation is isothermal. The additional heat supplied, and therefore the increase of entropy, will be in proportion to the dryness fraction. The tables showing the properties of steam and other gases give their pressures for each temperature, the different values for $\frac{d\,p}{d\,t}$, and other constants, such as the specific weight, or the inverse of the specific volume u' of the steam. Most of these data have been determined by experiments, though some have been deduced from calculation, according to a method to be explained later. In the tables in the Appendix sufficient information will be found for tracing diagrams, but more detailed tables are of course required for scientific calculations.

XVI. *Entropy Diagram.*—As the form of the curves depends on the nature of the liquid, we will first study the diagram for steam, Fig. 15. As before, the absolute temperatures are taken as ordinates, and the entropy for one kilo. of water at zero° C., or 273° absolute, is assumed to be nil. From Table **III** (in Appendix) the entropy curve for water is easily plotted, the successive points on which represent the condition

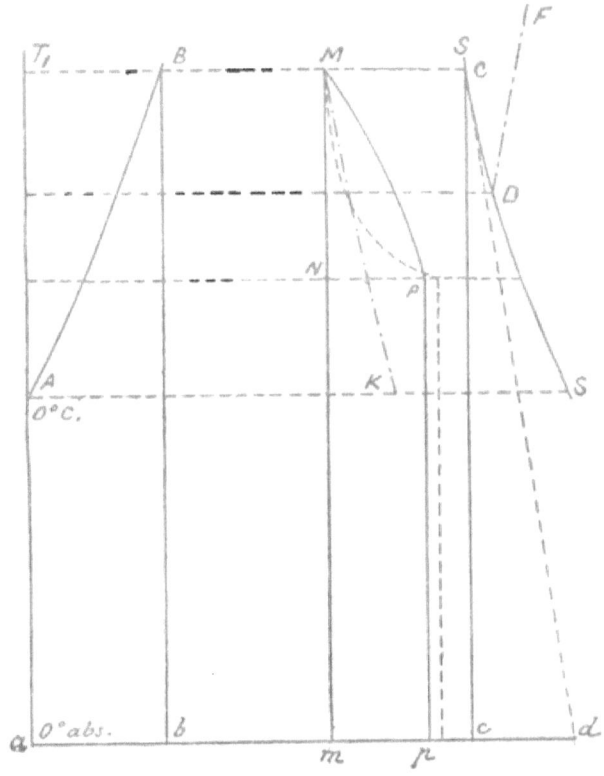

FIG. 15.—ENTROPY DIAGRAM FOR WATER AND **STEAM**.

of the water at increasing temperatures. The curve S S to the right of A B is obtained by plotting the values of $\frac{r}{T}$ for each temperature, and the different points on it represent the condition of dry saturated steam at these temperatures. The quantity of heat required, q, to heat one kilo. of water at 0° C. to the temperature T_1 and the corresponding pressure, is represented by the area a A B b. From point B at temperature T_1 the water begins to evaporate, and the state of the mixture of

steam and water (or its entropy) is marked by successive points along
the isothermal line B C. The latent heat r is represented by the rectangle b B C c. The total heat, or λ, is the sum of the two areas, and
increases slowly with the rise in temperature, since

$$\lambda = 606 \cdot 5 + 0 \cdot 305\, t.$$

The dryness fraction x of the mixture is in proportion to the heat
supplied from point B onwards, that is to $r\,x$. Any point M between
B and C shows the state of the mixture, corresponding to a dryness
fraction

$$x = \frac{\mathrm{B\,M}}{\mathrm{B\,C}} \, .$$

Thus, if the dryness fraction is known for the successive temperatures during a change of state, it may be represented by the entropy curve M P,
which reveals at once the quantity of heat supplied or withdrawn along
the expansion line M P. The dryness fraction varies with the position
of M upon the line B C. Thus, if the initial steam be very dry, that is
the dryness fraction = unity (point C), adiabatic expansion will make
it fall below unity with decreasing temperature, and cause partial condensation. If the dryness fraction is *nil* (point B), adiabatic expansion
will generate steam, as happens when hot water flows under pressure
from a boiler. On the other hand, if a mixture with a low dryness
fraction be compressed adiabatically, it will return to a liquid condition
with increased temperature.

To maintain the condition of saturation realised at point C with
decreasing temperature or pressure, a certain quantity of heat must be
supplied to it, as shown by the curve S S. The specific heat L during
expansion of the steam will be

$$\mathrm{L} = \frac{d\,\mathrm{Q}}{d\,\mathrm{T}} = \mathrm{T}\,\frac{d\,\mathrm{S}}{d\,\mathrm{T}} \, .$$

S being the entropy for dry saturated steam at the absolute temperature T, we get

$$\mathrm{S} = \int_{o}^{t} l\,\frac{d\,t}{\mathrm{T}} + \frac{r}{\mathrm{T}} \, .$$

Calculating from this the value of $\dfrac{d\,\mathrm{S}}{d\,\mathrm{T}}$, and substituting it for the value
of L, we have

$$\mathrm{L} = l + \frac{\mathrm{T}\,d\,\dfrac{r}{\mathrm{T}}}{d\,\mathrm{T}} = l + \frac{d\,r}{d\,\mathrm{T}} - \frac{r}{\mathrm{T}},$$

which is the value given by Clausius for the specific heat of saturated steam. According to par. IX, L is the subtangent $c\,d$ (Fig. 15), and is positive for decreasing values of T.

If heat be supplied to dry saturated steam, and the pressure maintained constant, the steam becomes superheated, and can, as stated in par. XV, be treated as a permanent gas, of which the specific heat C at constant pressure is = 0·48. The change of state is represented by a line **D F**, of the same kind as A B, but in which the entropy abscissæ increase only half as rapidly. The temperature of superheated steam at constant pressure rises rapidly for a very small expenditure of heat; the principal difficulties in generating it are caused by the slow rate of transmission of heat through a mass of steam, and by the slight convection of the gases and the walls.

Most gases behave in the same way as steam, and their line of saturation inclines to the right, Fig. 16. Ether forms an exception, and possesses the well-known property of becoming superheated by adiabatic expansion, and condensed by compression.

It is easy to solve many theoretical problems by means of the entropy diagram, such as finding the curves of constant dryness fraction, etc. The usual equation giving the dryness fraction at the different stages of adiabatic expansion may be found by taking the entropy of the adiabatic M N, Fig. 15, as a constant; and we then have

$$\int_0^{T_1} \frac{d\,q}{T} + \frac{r_1 x_1}{T_1} = \int_0^{T_2} \frac{d\,q}{T} + \frac{r_2 x_2}{T_2},$$

from which we get x_2 or the dryness fraction at temperature T_2, corresponding to x_1, dryness fraction of the steam at the initial temperature T_1.

When the expansion line M P is not adiabatic, the increase of entropy is calculated from the heat supplied, and is represented by N P, or

$$\int_{T_1}^{T_2} \frac{d\,Q}{T}.$$

x'_2 being the dryness fraction at point P, we have

$$\int_0^{T_2} \frac{d\,q}{T} + \frac{r_2 x'_2}{T_2} = \int_0^{T_1} \frac{d\,q}{T} + \frac{r_1 x_1}{T_1} + \int_{T_1}^{T_2} \frac{d\,Q}{T}.$$

To calculate the last integral of the above equation, it is not sufficient to know the total heat supplied during expansion, that is the area $m\,M\,P\,p$; for many equivalent areas may be traced, corresponding to different variations in entropy, as shown by the one in dotted lines.

XVII. *Expansion of Steam in contact with a metal plate.*—We will suppose that a very thin sheet of iron, weighing *m* kilos., is immersed in the kilo. of expanding mixture, and at each instant acquires its temperature.

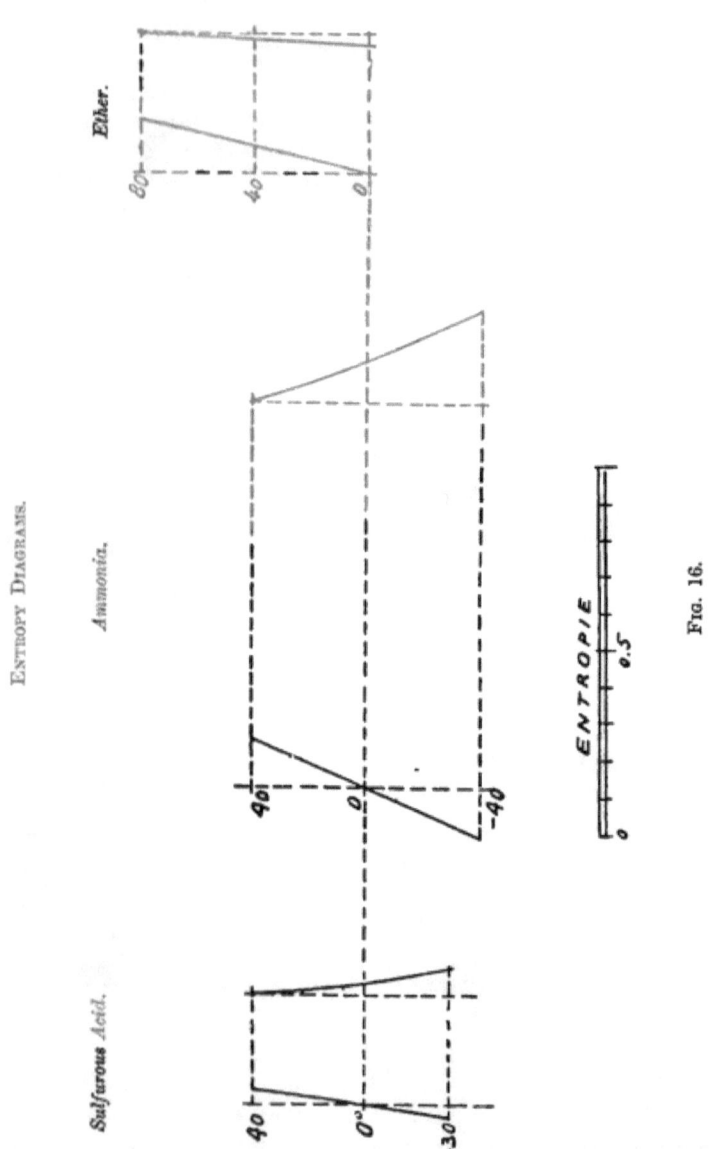

Fig. 16.

The problem is to find the expansion curve and the corresponding dryness fraction of the steam.

If C_1 be the specific heat of the iron, the heat supplied to the expanding mixture for the diminution of temperature $d\,T$ is

$$- m\,C_1\,d\,T,$$

and the increase of entropy of the fluid is

$$d\,S = - m\,C_1\,\frac{d\,T}{T},$$

or by integration

$$\int_{T_1}^{T} d\,S = m\,C_1 \log_e \frac{T_1}{T}.$$

This curve is shown at M K, Fig. 15, and is of the same class as the entropy curve for water A B, the only change being that the abscissæ must be multiplied by $m\,C_1$. (The specific heat of water is taken as = unity.) For example, let us trace the diagram for steam with an initial dryness fraction of 70 per cent., and a fall in temperature from 175° C. or about 8 atmospheres pressure, to 100° C. or atmospheric pressure. One kilo. of the mixture would then fill at admission a cylinder having 32 inches diameter and 5 feet stroke. The wrought-iron plate is supposed to be circular, and to have the same area as the piston, and a thickness of $\frac{1}{25}$ inch. We then get the values

$$m = 3\cdot9 \text{ kilos. } C_1 = 0\cdot13. \quad m\,C_1 = 0\cdot507,$$

and from measurement of the diagram we may calculate as follows:

Dryness fraction after adiabatic expansion, 66 per cent.

Dryness fraction after expansion, as affected by the iron plate, $72\cdot5$ per cent.

Thus the heat imparted to the mixture by the iron plate increases the dryness fraction and the external work done during expansion, and also, as shown by the entropy diagram, the internal latent heat of the mixture.

XVIII. *Volume of Saturated Steam and Expansion Curve in the p v Diagram.*—We have already seen that the volume u' of the steam has been obtained by calculation, and not from direct experiment. It can be determined by a formula known as Clapeyron's equation, which will be deduced from the entropy diagram, by means of a method first employed by M. Mollier.[*]

---

[*] 'Das Wärmediagramm,' by R. Mollier, Berlin, Simion (publisher), 1893.

The $p\,v$ diagram for any fluid, Fig. 17, consists of the line of constant volume u of the liquid, its expansion being neglected, and the saturation curve, the abscissæ of which are u'. Thus we may consider the

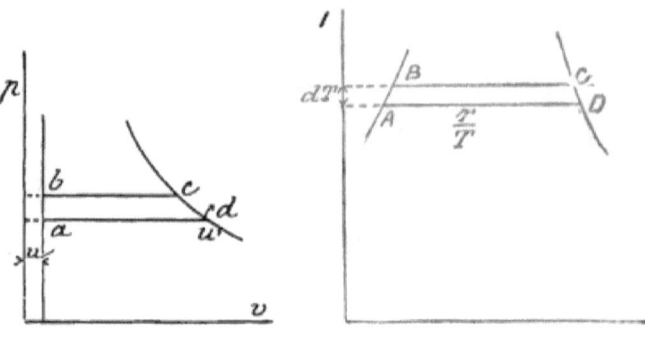

FIG. 17.

small cycle $a\ b\ c\ d$ as carried out between two temperatures differing by d T, the difference of pressures being $d\,p$. The heat converted into work in this cycle is $A\,(u' - u)\dfrac{d\,p}{d\,T}\,d\,T$, and is equivalent to the area $a\,b\,c\,d$.

We will now draw the entropy diagram A B C D to represent the same cycle. The heat will be expressed by

$$\frac{r}{T}\,d\,T,$$

and we get the equation

$$r = A\ T\ \frac{d\,p}{d\,T}\,(u' - u)\,;$$

r, p, and $\dfrac{d\,p}{d\,T}$ being known from Regnault's tables for different values of T. As u is the volume of the liquid, we can from this equation calculate u' and thus the inverse ratio or specific weight γ of the steam. If expansion is not complete, the volume of wet steam is

$$u + (u' - u)\,x,$$

and the increase of entropy is $\dfrac{r\,x}{T}$. As both members of the last equation have to be multiplied by the factor x, the same equation is still applicable.

The expansion curve in the $p\,v$ diagram is easily traced, because, from the volumes u' given in the tables, the saturation curve S S, Fig. 18, can be drawn. To find the point *m* corresponding to the dryness fraction *x*, *b c* must be so divided that

$$\frac{b\,m}{b\,c} = x.$$

The dryness fraction being known from the entropy diagram, the expansion curve may be determined from it.

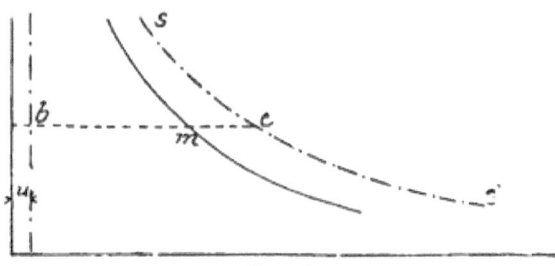

FIG. 18.

XIX. *Geometrical Relation between the p v and the Entropy Diagrams.*— In Fig. 19, L L is the entropy line for water, S S is the line of saturation for steam, the curve drawn to the left of the entropy diagram is the pressure curve for saturated steam, the vertical ordinates being the temperatures as before. Thus R is a point in the curve of pressures, and a tangent carried through it gives the value $\frac{d\,p}{d\,T}$ for temperature T_3. The triangle M N K, obtained by drawing M K parallel to this tangent, gives

$$N K = \frac{M N}{\frac{d p}{d T}} = \frac{r}{T\,\frac{d p}{d T}}.$$

Calculating this value from the equation in paragraph XVIII we get

$$N K = A\,(u' - u).$$

Again, if a point *n* be selected, corresponding to a dryness fraction *x* which is less than unity, we have

$$n\,k = A\,(u' - u)\,x.$$

Each point along a line of expansion D D, or along the line of saturated steam S S, may be thus treated, but it will be found more convenient to have the same basis for all the triangles, namely the horizontal line passing through 0° C. This may be taken as the origin of an axis directed downwards, which serves as the axis of volumes.

Quantities such as N K can then be transferred horizontally and furnish corresponding points as N_1. The lengths $M_1 N_1$, $M_1 n_1$ equal to N K, $n k$ represent the expansion $u' - u$, or $(u' - u)\,x$ of the fluid from a liquid

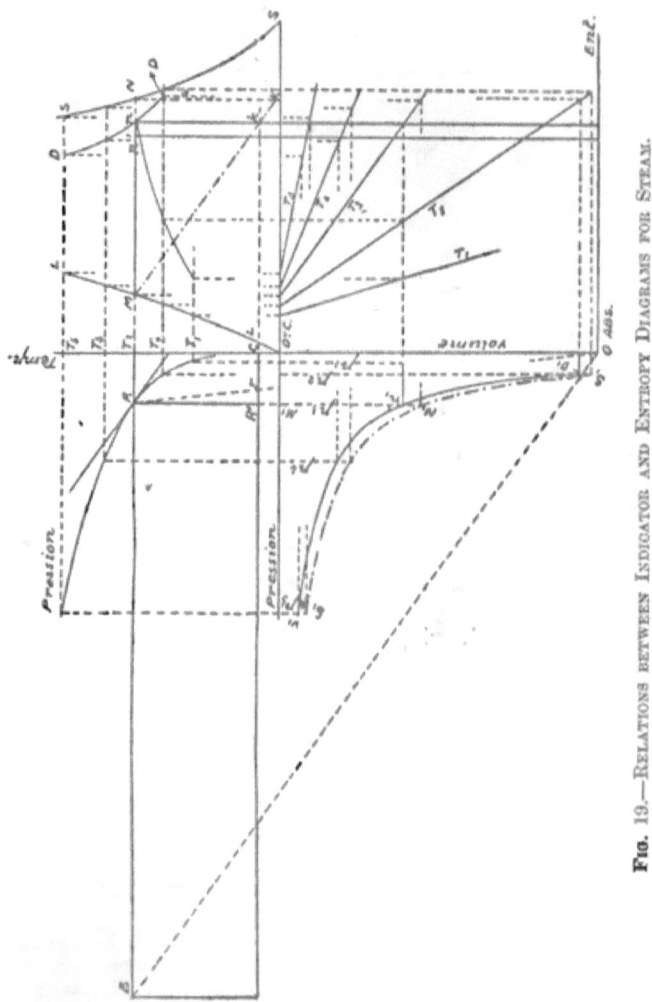

FIG. 19.—RELATIONS BETWEEN INDICATOR AND ENTROPY DIAGRAMS FOR STEAM.

state until the steam is partially or wholly evaporated, the factor A being eliminated by the scale of the drawing. The volume u of the water may be neglected when considering ordinary pressures, and replaced by adding A u to A $(u' - u)$ or A $(u' - u)\,x$. This can be done by slightly **shifting** upwards **the** base line **from which the** volumes are measured; then the vertical ordinates if **carried downwards will** give the volumes of saturated **steam,** or of the mixture **here** considered. The factor Λ is always omitted, and only taken into account when determining the scale of the volumes. If all points such as *n* on the entropy line D D are thus treated, they will furnish a continuous line $D_1 D_1$, forming the expansion curve in the *p v* diagram.

It would be rather difficult to draw accurately **the tangents to the** pressure curve without the **help** of the values of $\dfrac{d\,p}{d\,T}$, **which are given in** the table of properties of **steam in** the Appendix. The pressures are calculated **by** Regnault **and Zeuner** in millimetres of mercury, and have been converted in **these tables** into **kilos.** per square metre. This graphic method will **be found** very convenient, because the diagram, with all **its** temperature lines, pressure curves, entropy curves L L and S S, and tangents T_1, T_2 .... T_s, may be **drawn** once for all or lithographed, and an entropy converted into a *p v* line, **or** *vice versâ*, without any **calculation,** simply by **means of a** few parallel vertical and horizontal lines. **Thus, to trace the adiabatic *p v* curve, it** is merely necessary to cut all the tangents T_1, etc., by a vertical, and **to** transfer the points, where they **intersect each other, horizontally on to the lines** of pressure. It is equally **easy to transpose the *p v* to the entropy diagram.** To get **the** line of **constant volume passing through *n* in the T S system, we** draw a horizontal passing **through *n_1* in the *p v* diagram, and shift vertically** the points where it intersects the tangents T_1 .... T_s.

The diagram, Fig. 19, **shows other** relations **between** the properties **of a gas** which it may **be** useful to describe. Thus, if O B be drawn **parallel to the tangent at** R, and passes through **the** absolute zero, the **triangle O B T_3 gives**

$$T_3\,B = T\,\frac{d\,p}{d\,T}.$$

Now

$$C\,T_3 = n\,k = A\,(u' - u)\,x.$$

Therefore the area of the rectangle B C is

$$A\,T\,\frac{d\,p}{d\,T}\,(u' - u)\,x,$$

or *r x* (see paragraph XVIII), while the area of the rectangle R C is

$$A\,p\,(u' - u)\,x.$$

The rectangle B C or $r\,x$ represents the total latent heat of evaporation, or the heat absorbed by the fluid as it passes from a liquid state to the condition of the steam shown at point n (dryness fraction x). R C is the latent heat converted into external work during evaporation; the difference between the two represents the heat equivalent to the internal work done. If we join O R we see by the proportion between the triangles R R'r and O R T$_3$ that the rectangle R C, or latent heat converted into external work, is equal to one having R'r as a base and the height T$_3$, therefore R'r is the entropy corresponding to the heat converted into external work in the process of evaporation at constant pressure. If this be represented by the line $n\,n'$, the total entropy M n consists of M n', corresponding to the internal latent heat, and of $n'\,n$.

For practical use the scale of volumes must now be calculated. This should be carried out in such a way that M$_1$ N$_1$ represents the volume $u' - u$, that is, the excess of the volume of dry saturated steam over that of water at the absolute temperature T$_3$; this volume is deduced from the specific weight of steam in the tables. For example, let T$_3$ correspond to 100° C. or 373° absolute (boiling point), a temperature at which a cubic metre of steam weighs 0·606 kilo., then the volume of one kilo. will be

$$u' = \frac{1}{0\cdot606},$$

$$M_1 N_1 = u' - u = \frac{1}{0\cdot606} - 0\cdot001 = 1\cdot649 \text{ cubic metres.}$$

We may have to start from an actual indicator diagram with any weight of mixture, for converting it into an entropy curve. Let us first suppose the weight of mixture to be one kilo., and the dryness fraction known for one point. The volume $(u' - u)\,x$ may then be calculated, and drawn at M$_1$ n_1 to the same scale as M$_1$ N. This gives one point n_1 of the indicator curve, from which the others can be determined, and the entropy curve traced. The actual weight may now be calculated, by multiplying the entropy scale by the ratio between unity and the actual weight of fluid used in the cycle. We shall come back to this question hereafter in paragraph XXVIII.

XX. *Remarks on the Law of Expansion of Steam.*—To calculate the dimensions of steam engine cylinders for a given power, it is usual to select a hypothetical law of expansion, that is, a simple geometrical curve from which, although not perhaps very accurate, calculations can easily be made. The common hyperbola answers this purpose well, as long as the efficiency is not deduced from it, because it so far agrees with actual expansion and compression curves, that an engineer who applies it will not be led to make an engine cylinder much too large or too small. For-

merly this common hyperbolic curve used to be compared with the actual
expansion curve, as shown on an indicator diagram, and their points of
agreement noted. It is an interesting study to find the entropy curve
corresponding to the *p v* hyperbolic curve for any given dryness fraction.
They are shown in Fig. 20 for dryness fractions of 30 per cent. to 90 per
cent. For very wet steam the hyperbolic expansion curve does not
differ much from the adiabatic, at pressures varying from 8 to 1 atmosphere absolute. If the dryness fraction is above 40 per cent., the
hyperbolic expansion curve shows that much heat has been refunded
from the walls. In actual steam engines a low dryness fraction at cut-
off means that, owing to the cooling down of the walls during the preceding expansion and exhaust stroke, much heat is withdrawn from the
steam and absorbed by the walls. On the other hand, a high percentage
of steam at cut-off causes the expansion curve to be nearer the adiabatic.
If the indicator diagram furnishes a hyperbolic expansion curve, the dryness fraction at cut-off will often average 60 or 70 per cent. For a lower
dryness fraction the expansion would be above the hyperbolic.

XXI. *Diagrams of* CO_2 *marking the Critical* Point.—Carbonic acid, a
gas which becomes superheated at ordinary temperature and pressure,
has not been as thoroughly and accurately studied as steam, but enough
is known about its characteristics to justify the application to it, for
ordinary practical purposes, of the data already obtained. From the
values given by Regnault and Zeuner (see Table IV in the Appendix)
and the volume of the liquid gas at different temperatures and pressures, as determined by Cailletet and Mathias, the diagram, Fig. 21, has
been constructed, the method followed being the same as for steam.

The first peculiarity which strikes us in this diagram is the flat
gradient of the entropy curve of the liquid, caused by its rapid increase
in specific heat, and its intersection at a very low temperature, $31 \cdot 9^\circ$ C.,
with the curve of saturation. The volume of the liquid is very large
compared to that of the gas, and this volume, instead of varying very
slightly, as it does for water, increases greatly for a small temperature
range. The intersection of the entropy curves for CO_2 as a liquid and
as a gas marks a well-known condition common to both, called the critical
point. This point exists also for steam, but it is too high to be shown
within the limits of our diagram, or found by means of Regnault's data,
on which it is based. For gases which liquefy with difficulty the critical
point lies much below temperatures easily attained by means of a refrigerator. Carbonic acid, which stands on the boundary line midway
between vapours and permanent gases, well illustrates the processes of
liquefaction.

We will suppose that a kilo. of CO_2 at 0° C. is maintained in a liquid

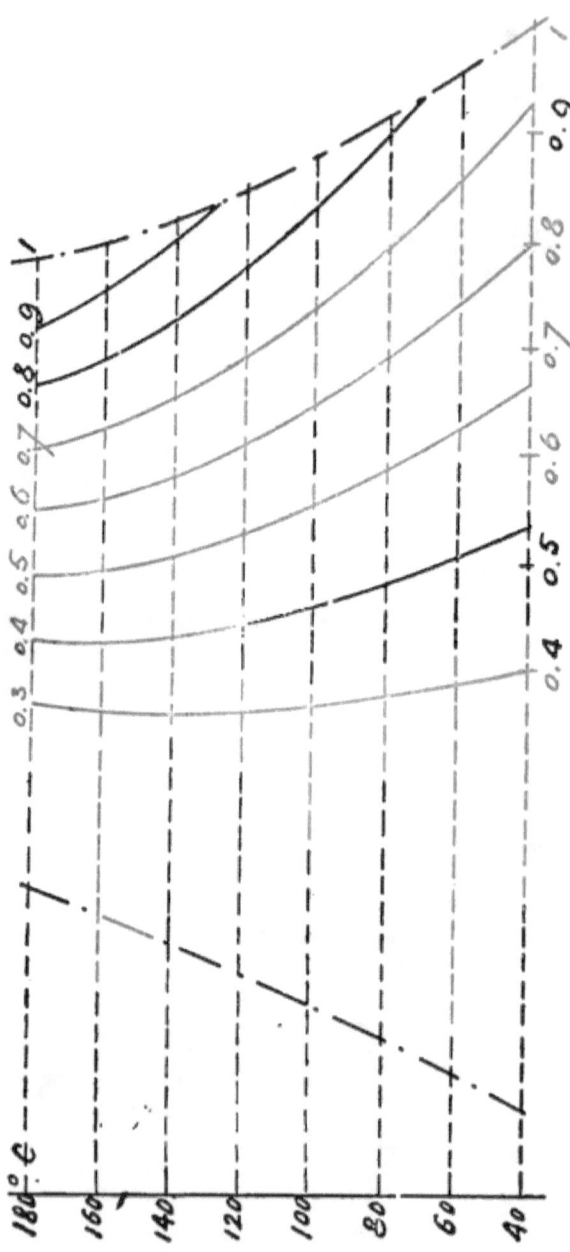

FIG. 20.—ENTROPY LINES FOR HYPERBOLIC EXPANSION OF WET STEAM.

condition at the corresponding pressure, or about 35 atmospheres. If at this pressure 56·28 calories are communicated to it, it evaporates completely to a dry saturated gas, and if more heat is imparted to it at the same pressure it becomes superheated, and the temperature rises. The superheat is shown in the diagram by a line similar to one already described in paragraph VIII. (heating a gas at constant pressure).

If, on the other hand, we take the gas at ordinary temperature and pressure, compress it at this temperature to 35 atmospheres, and cool it at the same pressure by withdrawing heat from it, the temperature will fall. When it has sunk to 0° C. the gas will have parted with all its superheat, and become a saturated vapour. If the abstraction of heat at the same pressure be continued the gas will liquefy until condensation is complete. Heat may be still further withdrawn from it, if the pressure be reduced, and the carbonic acid will continue liquid.

The gas may be also liquefied by another process shown on the entropy diagram, Fig. 21, namely by isothermal compression starting from ordinary temperature and pressure. Heat being thus abstracted from it, the gas will reach the condition of saturated vapour and then that of a liquid. The pressure will be higher, but no refrigerator will be required to effect the process, water at ordinary temperature, or even the external air, being sufficient to produce the cooling, if compression be carried out very slowly. It is, however, essential in this isothermal liquefaction that it be effected at a temperature below the critical point; in other words, that the horizontal line representing this isothermal process on the entropy diagram should cut the curves both of the liquid and of the saturated gas. These phenomena explain why permanent gases cannot be liquefied by compression only. The pressure must be accompanied by a fall in temperature produced either by a refrigerator, or by the sudden expansion of the compressed and cooled gas.

XXII. *Expansion of Wet Steam when mixed with a Permanent Gas.*— This condition is produced in air compressors with water injections, in the air pumps of steam engine condensers, and in some other cases.

Let m be the weight of gas per kilo. of the mixture of steam and water. We will assume that an instantaneous exchange of heat takes place between them, that all are at the same temperature, and finally that the gas is neither dissolved in the water nor combines chemically with it. During expansion and exchange of heat between the mixture of water and steam and the gas, the entropy of the one diminishes as that of the other increases, so that the sum of the entropy of both remains constant if the change of state is adiabatic, and if otherwise it varies by a given amount. Let M N, Fig. 22, be the line of change of state for the mixture of steam and water, T_1 being the initial, and T any given temperature, the volumes of steam at T_1 and T will be

$$v_1 = ab \qquad v = cd.$$

These are the respective volumes of the weight m of the permanent gas at the said temperatures, because according to Dalton's law water evaporates in a vessel filled with gas as in a vacuum, and the pressure of

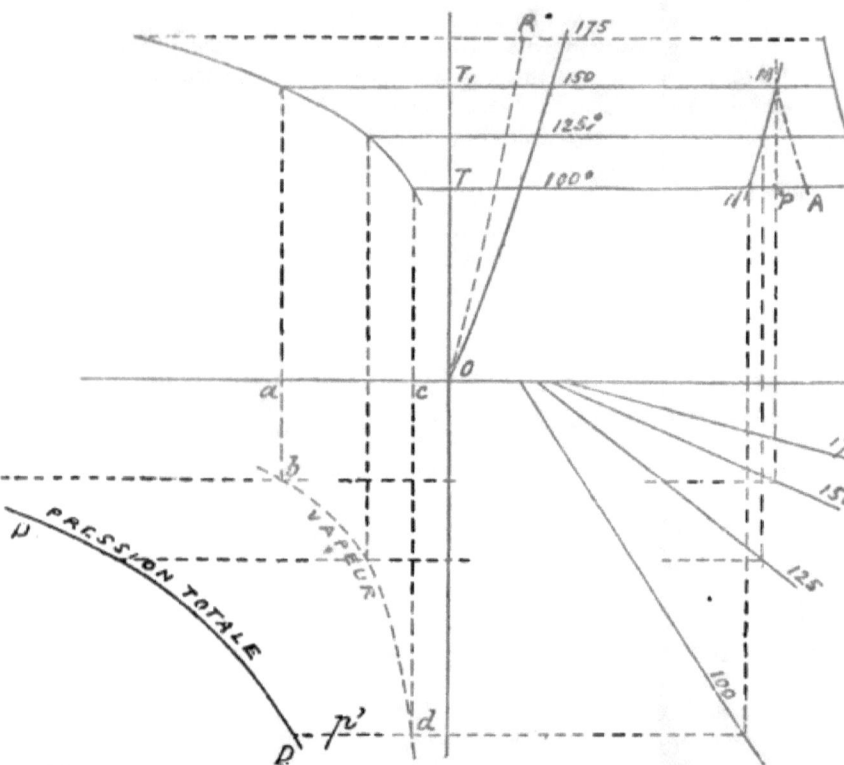

FIG. 22.—MIXTURE OF STEAM WITH PERMANENT GASES.

steam for a given temperature is the same, whether there is gas in the vessel or not. Now, the increase of entropy in a gas during any change of state is (paragraph VII.)

$$S - S_1 = - m c \log_e \frac{T}{T_1} + m (C - c) \log_e \frac{v}{v_1}.$$

If the process for steam, water and air is adiabatic we have

$$N P = S - S_1;$$

or, from the preceding equation,

$$m\,(C - c)\,\log_\epsilon \frac{v}{v_1} = N\,P + m\,c\,\log_\epsilon \frac{T}{T_1}.$$

The last term of this equation may be calculated, and the corresponding variation in entropy is shown by the differences in the horizontal ordinates of the curve O R. The direction of this curve may be reversed, it may be drawn from M to A and the above equation thus written :

$$m\,(C - c)\,\log_\epsilon \frac{v}{v_1} = N\,A.$$

Having traced the curve M A, a fictitious position must at first be assigned to point N, and corrected afterwards to agree with the equation, the ratio $\frac{v}{v_1}$ $\left(\text{or } \frac{c\,d}{a\,b}\right)$ depending on the position of N.

The total pressure in the cylinder is found by adding the pressure of the gas, p', to that of the steam. The weight m and temperature T being known, and the volume v of the gas determined from the volume of the steam, the pressure p' of the gas is given by the fundamental equation (see paragraph VII)

$$p'\,v = m\,R\,T.$$

Pressure p' being thus found, it is added in the $p\,v$ diagram to the horizontal ordinate of point d, and thus we obtain the expansion curve D D). It will be seen from the diagram that if the mixture be adiabatically compressed, the dryness fraction increases, and is finally equal to unity; beyond this point the steam becomes superheated, and the enclosed fluids behave approximately as a mixture of the two gases would do. We may conclude that if air be mixed with steam, a more rapid condensation during expansion will be produced than if steam alone is present in a cylinder.

XXIII. *Flow of Steam.*—Let us suppose a mixture of steam and water to flow from one reservoir, where the pressure is p_1 and dryness fraction x_1, into another in which the pressure is p_2 less than p_1; let x_2 be the dryness fraction

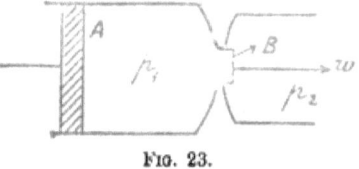

Fig. 23.

and v the speed of the steam at the contracted mouth of the orifice. We will assume that no heat is communicated to the steam in its passage from one reservoir to the other.

Take two sections of the reservoirs, A and B, Fig. 23, and consider what takes place between them during a very small space of time $d\,\mathfrak{T}$. The energy which acts upon the fluid enclosed within these two sections is produced for one part by pressures p_1 and p_2, and for the other part is liberated by the fluid during the time $d\,\mathfrak{T}$. According to the principle of equivalence, the energy of motion acquired by the fluid is equivalent to that produced by pressures p_1 and p_2, and to the heat set free as the fluid passes from A to B. Thus we obtain the equation

$$A\,\frac{w_2}{2\,g} = A\,(p_1 - p_2)\,u + q_1 - q_2 + r_1\,x_1 - r_2\,x_2\,;$$

the first member of which expresses as heat the energy of motion of the fluid passing into the vessel B. The term $A\,(p_1 - p_2)\,u$ representing the heat equivalent to the work of driving out the fluid in a liquid state from the high-pressure to the low-pressure reservoir, is very small and often neglected for practical purposes. The dryness fraction x_2 may be calculated from x_1, assuming that the fluid expands adiabatically from A to B. In the entropy diagram, Fig. 24, the second member of this equation is represented by the sum of the shaded areas, while by exaggerating the volume u, it has been possible to show the first term in the small horizontal area to the left on the pressure diagram. By neglecting these small figures, the kinetic energy will be represented as heat by the shaded area to the right only.

After the jet of steam is discharged into the low-pressure reservoir, its speed is diminished by friction and eddies against the stationary gas. The energy of motion $A\,\dfrac{w_2}{2\,g}$ is again transformed into heat, but the temperature remains constant, as long as the dryness fraction is below unity. If x'_2 be this fraction then

$$A\,\frac{w_2}{2\,g} = r_2\,(x'_2 - x_2).$$

The condition of the mixture of steam and water will be shown by the point P on the entropy diagram, Fig. 24, by taking

$$N\,P = \frac{r_2\,(x'_2 - x_2)}{T_2},$$

or making the rectangle $N\,P\,p\,n$ equal to the sum of the two shaded areas.

When the initial dryness fraction in the first reservoir is very high, as for point M', the final point F will be beyond the saturation curve, showing that the fluid is superheated. The position of point F gives the temperature of superheat. **As shown in this diagram, a fluid** flowing **through an** orifice **cannot be superheated unless the initial dryness fraction** is nearly equal **to unity. If** this is the case, and the tem-

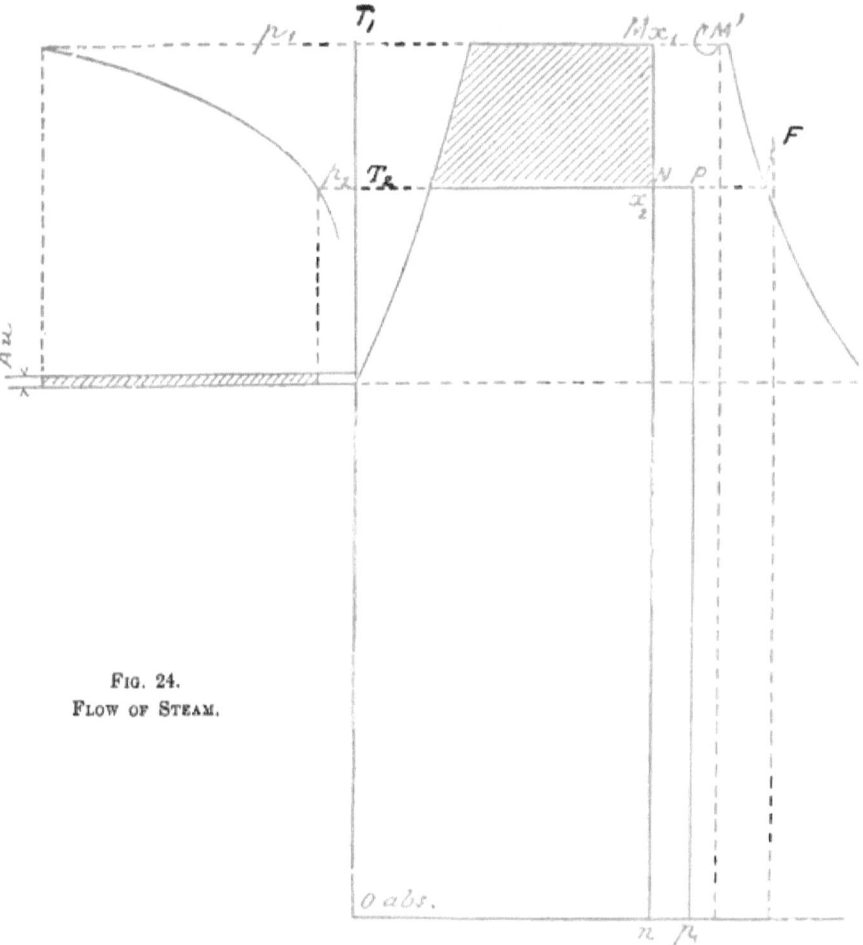

Fig. 24.
Flow of Steam.

perature of superheat is known from experiment, the point **F** denoting it will be given on the diagram, **M'** can be calculated from it, and the original dryness fraction found.

This is the principle on which the Peabody calorimeter for determining the dryness fraction or quality of the steam in a boiler or pipe is based. The apparatus consists first of a small separating reservoir to collect the

larger part of the priming water, that the steam, thus partially freed
from moisture, may be superheated in flowing through an orifice. The
water collected in the separator is weighed, and also that produced by
condensing the superheated steam in a refrigerating coil. From the sum
of these two· weights, and the temperature of superheat taken with an
accurate thermometer, the dryness fraction of the steam is easily
determined.

CHAPTER VI.

STEAM ENGINES.

XXIV. *Cycle of a Steam Engine.*—In the diagram, Fig. 25, the essential parts of a steam engine are shown : G being the boiler, C the single-
acting cylinder, *a* the admission, *e* the exhaust valve, *c* the surface
condenser, *p* the air pump worked from the engine, *t* the steam pipe, *r* the

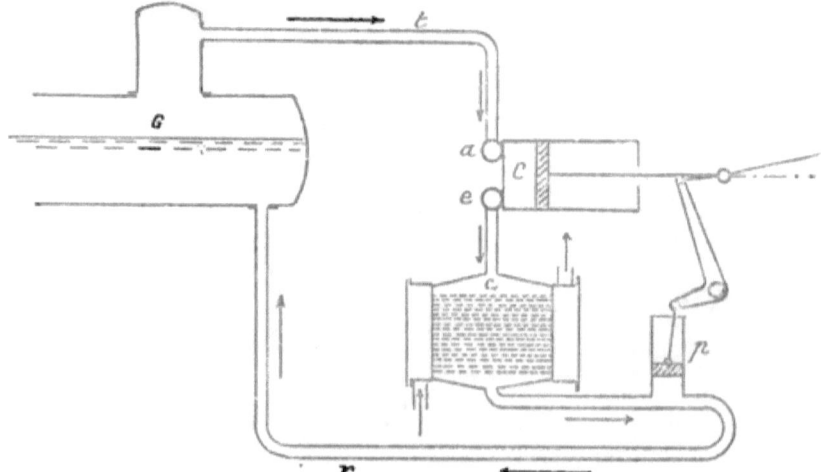

FIG. 25.—STEAM ENGINE CYCLE.

feed pipe to return the condensation water to the boiler. In a surface
condensing engine the air pump and the feed pump may be considered
as one in theory, although in actual work the pressure of the water
withdrawn from the condenser is first raised by an air pump to atmo-

sphere, and then forced by a feed pump into the boiler.* The successive operations carried out in a boiler, cylinder, condenser and pump, combine to produce a cycle, which we will now study in detail.

The working fluid leaves the boiler as a mixture of steam and water at a temperature T_1 absolute, its dryness fraction x_1 being in most cases very high. After passing through the phases of the cycle it is returned to the boiler as water, at temperature T_2. Neglecting all loss of pressure, friction in the pipes, or conduction, external or internal, from the walls, we see that the fluid admitted passes through a cycle inferior to those described in paragraphs V. and VI. as far as efficiency is concerned. But, as the above conditions cannot be obtained in practice,

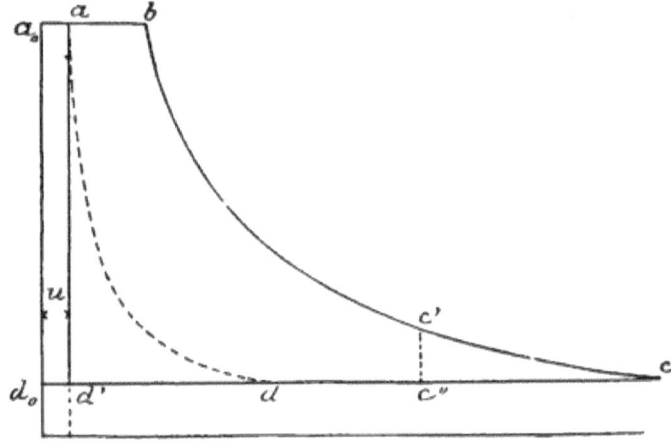

Fig. 26.—Ideal Indicator Diagram.

the cycle is ideal. We need not take the pump which circulates the cooling water into account, because the duty of this pump is only to overcome the friction of the water, and it affects the mechanical efficiency in the same way as the frictional resistance of the piston, valves, &c.

The work done on the motor piston is represented by the area $a_o\, b\, c\, d_o$, Fig. 26, expansion is complete, and there is no clearance volume. Part of this work is absorbed by the air and feed pumps p, to raise the volume u of the condensed water from pressure p_2 of the condenser to pressure p_1 of the boiler; this is represented on the diagram by the rectangle $a_o\, a\, d'\, d_o$. Thus the net work done on the piston is the re-

---

* The case of a surface condenser is here considered, but our remarks would apply equally to a jet condenser.

maining area *a b c d'*. The water is heated in the boiler from temperature T_2 to temperature T_1, and is converted into steam of dryness
fraction x_1. The heat supplied to the water is thus

$$q_1 - q_2 + r_1\, x_1.$$

Although the consecutive operations for turning heat into work are
carried out by different organs, they may be considered as the successive
phases of a closed cycle, comprising :

1. *a b.*—Evaporation of the liquid charge at temperature T_1 into
steam of dryness fraction x_1, the result being work at constant pressure
done on the piston.

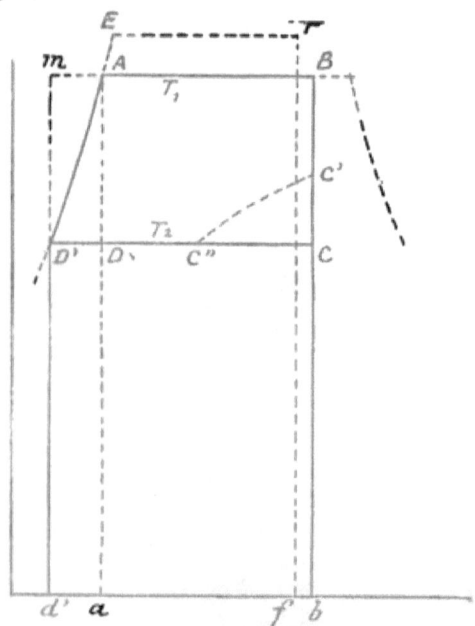

Fig. 27.—Ideal Entropy Diagram.

2. *b c.*—Adiabatic expansion of the mixture of steam and water
between temperatures T_1 and T_2.

3. *c d'.*—Condensation at constant pressure p_2 of the steam contained
in the mixture at point *c*.

4. *d' a.*—Supplying heat to the water from the source of heat between
temperatures T_2 and T_1.

This closed cycle, *a b c d'*, differs from Carnot's, because the fluid
returns to its initial condition by the external application of heat, and

not by adiabatic compression. The cycle might be improved by substituting the dotted line *d a* of adiabatic compression for *d d' a*. The area of the diagram would be smaller, less heat being withdrawn from the boiler, a larger fraction would be turned into work, and the thermal efficiency would be higher, as demonstrated in paragraph V. Practically, however, no advantage would be thus obtained, because the boiler being fed with water at temperature T_1, no heat could be abstracted from the gases of combustion when leaving the boiler flues. In other words, if Carnot's cycle were used, it would not be possible to derive any benefit from a feed water heater.

The entropy diagram shows the efficiency of the ideal engine here considered. The same operations are lettered alike in the *p v* diagram, Fig. 26, and the entropy diagram, Fig. 27. In the latter, following the same order as before, we have :

1. A B.—Evaporation of the fluid, necessitating the application of heat shown by the rectangle *a* A B *b*.

2. B C.—Adiabatic expansion. ·

3. C D'.—Condensation with abstraction of heat represented by the area *d'* D' C *b*.

4. D' A.—Supply of heat to the water in the boiler, shown by the area *d'* D' A *a*. Thus the heat turned into work is D' A B C, and the thermal efficiency of the cycle is

$$U = \frac{D' A B C}{d' D' A B b}.$$

It is not difficult to demonstrate, from the shape of the areas of Fig. 27, certain propositions generally arrived at by laborious calculations, such as the effect of initial pressure, dryness fraction of the steam, etc., on the efficiency of the engine. Thus we can see at a glance that the efficiency of the cycle here considered is less than that of a Carnot cycle between the same limits of temperature, which is

$$\frac{D'' A B C}{a A B b},$$

because of the inclination of the line D' A. This superiority will increase if A B be shorter, as it may be for wet steam or other gases. In the Carnot cycle all gases have the same efficiency, but this is not the case in the cycle here considered, where the water must be heated by the external application of heat.

The efficiency increases with the **initial temperature** *or pressure*, because, for the same expenditure of heat (area *d* D' E F *f*), the heat lost is less. The cycles in ordinary steam engine practice are affected by friction

E

in the pipes and throttling in the ports, and very greatly by the great conductivity of the walls.

Loss by Incomplete Expansion. — Let us suppose that expansion is stopped at c', Fig. 26, by opening the exhaust valve. The diagram is then completed by the lines $c'c''$ and $c''d'$, which no longer denote reversible operations, because the pressure of the steam is not balanced by an equal counterpressure. It is necessary, as before, to substitute an ideal process for the actual cycle of work, as shown by the indicator diagram.

We must first notice that the pv diagram will not be altered if $c'c''$ be taken as a line of condensation at constant volume, and $c''d'$ as one of condensation at constant pressure. These imaginary operations do not produce any change in the quantity of heat given up to the condenser, which always consists of the internal latent heat lost from c' to d', and of the heat equivalent to the work of compression by the piston during the exhaust stroke. These two quantities are alike in the actual and the imaginary process. By means of the latter we can follow the condition of the working fluid on the entropy diagram, and plot the line $C'C''$, Fig. 27, from the line of constant volume $c'c''$, Fig. 26, according to the method described in paragraph XIX.

XXV. *Effect of the Walls.*—The cylinder walls act by condensing part of the steam admitted upon their internal surfaces. As the temperature of the cycle decreases, heat is refunded by the walls to the fluid. In a complete cycle, with the exception of the external loss by radiation, and the heat supplied to the steam when the cylinder is jacketed, the sum of the exchanges of heat would be *nil*. The question, already studied at paragraph XVII, of the expansion of steam when in contact with a thin metal plate, is applicable to a certain extent to the wall action in an engine cylinder. We have mentioned it, as Professor Cotterill did, to show that the thermal efficiency diminishes, even when all the heat absorbed by the metal during admission is refunded during expansion. The analogy, however, must not be taken too far. The action of a thin plate surrounded by steam only roughly approximates to the thermal condition of the layer of metal in contact with the working fluid in a cylinder, the temperature of which varies with the time occupied by a stroke, and the depth from the inner surface of the metal. Professor Kirsch has studied this complex phenomenon analytically, and from another side serious attempts have been made to determine the actual cyclical temperatures at various depths and points in the cylinder walls and covers.* The practical results of such

---

* We refer to Mr. Bryan Donkin's experiments with small sensitive mercurial thermometers, and to the more recent researches by Professor Callendar to determine these high temperatures more accurately by means of an electric thermo-couple.

calculations and experiments would be to foretell the effect of wall action from the working conditions of a cylinder, its clearance surfaces, more or less complete jacketing, &c. We will not touch here upon this difficult question, our purpose being rather to deal with entropy diagrams and their application. Of course, the theory of steam engines will not be complete as long as we are obliged to content ourselves with taking the data of an accurate trial, and drawing up a heat balance from the results: but in many cases such an analysis will be found useful and may lead to improvements, principally as regards the designing of cylinders for economical engines. This is the reason why it is of practical importance to illustrate the utilisation of heat in steam engines by easy and graphic methods, although it must not be forgotten that these methods are, after all, based on assumptions more or less accurate. Following the example of Hirn, who founded the experimental method now universally employed, and others working on the same lines, we may state these hypotheses thus:

1. At the end of exhaust and beginning of compression, the cylinder contains no moisture or water, but only dry saturated steam.

2. At every point in the indicator diagram the fluid in the cylinder forms a homogeneous mixture at a uniform temperature.

3. At certain points of the cycle, as at cut-off and during expansion, the kinetic energy of the fluid is practically *nil*.

To draw up a heat balance, we require to know the shape of the indicator diagram, the weight of saturated steam admitted from the boiler per stroke at a given temperature and dryness fraction, weight of water condensed in the jacket, and the heat lost by radiation. The piston and valves ought to be steam-tight. If the engine is not working at constant pressure, cut-off, or speed, no true heat balance can be drawn, as the weight of steam is calculated from the mean of all the strokes; the same applies if the conditions are not the same on both faces of the piston. If, however, the load does not vary too much, a mean diagram can be obtained, sufficiently accurate for ordinary work. Before proceeding to apply the entropy diagram to an actual steam engine trial, we will treat our subject from a theoretical point of view, and elucidate a few difficulties which may arise on various points.

XXVI. *Clearance Space.*—Let us study an ordinary indicator curve, A B C D E F, Fig. 28. The clearance volume v, is known, as also the weight and dryness fraction of the mixture of steam and water coming from the boiler. To make the matter simpler, we will assume that this dryness fraction is equal to unity, as is often the case in practice. At point A on the diagram, the volume $A_o A$ is supposed to be dry saturated steam; the dryness fraction at point B can be calculated from the compression along A B, or determined by the graphic method. Let x_o be this dryness fraction, and μ the weight of fluid in the clearance as determined from its volume A_o A, and its pressure at the beginning of compression. The admission valve opens at point B, and the weight of steam y coming from the boiler is admitted at boiler pressure to fill the clearance. All constants for point B will be marked with subscript o, and those relating to the temperature and pressure of the boiler 1.

It is impossible to follow on an entropy diagram the thermal changes taking place from B to C; as the process is irreversible, the law of the mechanical equivalent is only applicable. Since no external work is done, the piston being at rest, the internal heat at point B, plus the heat

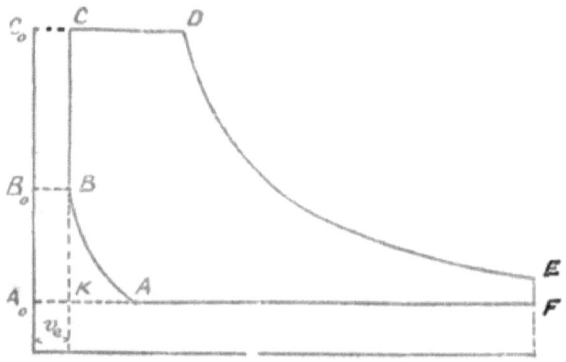

FIG. 28.—INDICATOR DIAGRAM WITH COMPRESSION.

supplied to the weight of steam y by the boiler, may be taken as equal to the internal heat of the weight $\mu + y$ in the clearance at boiler pressure. The dryness fraction x_1 is unknown at this point. Thus we have the equation

$$(1) \qquad \mu\,[q_o + x_o\,\{r_o - A\,p_o\,(u'_o - u)\}] + y\,(q_1 + r_1)$$
$$= (\mu + y)\,[q_1 + x_1\,\{r_1 - A\,p_1\,(u'_1 - u)\}].$$

Taking the weight of steam $\mu + y$ with dryness fraction x_1, the volume being that of the clearance space, we obtain a second equation

$$(2) \qquad (\mu + y)\,[u + x_1\,(u'_1 - u)] = v_o.$$

These two equations give the values of y and x_1.

Let P be the weight of steam admitted per stroke, and known from experiment. This weight includes the weight y to fill the clearance, already determined, and the remainder will be $P - y$. During operations B C and C D of the diagram, Fig. 28, part of the admission steam is condensed and goes to heat the walls. Thus at cut-off, point D, although the total weight of fluid during expansion is $\mu + P$, a certain part is already condensed. If the entropy diagram corresponding to this weight of steam be traced in the way indicated in paragraph XIX, and allowance made for incomplete expansion, paragraph XXIV, we get the diagram $A'_{\circ} C'_{\circ} D' E' F' A'_{\circ}$, corresponding to the $p\,v$ diagram $A_{\circ} C_{\circ} D E F A_{\circ}$. For the lines D E, E F of the indicator diagram we have D' E', E' F' on the entropy diagram, the weight of steam in both cases being $P + \mu$, and the processes of expansion and compression reversible.

But we may go further, because the total heat converted into work during the cycle may be found by supposing the indicator curve to represent a closed cycle (see paragraph XXIV) in which the constant weight $\mu + P$ is the agent. This weight of steam is supposed to remain in the cylinder, and to be alternately heated and cooled by external means (see paragraph XXIV). We will next trace the closed entropy diagram $A' B' C' D' E' F'$ (Fig. 29) by the graphic method described in paragraph XIX, equivalent to the work represented by A B C D E F, Fig. 28. The area of this closed cycle represents the heat turned into work per stroke, and can be compared with the area representing the heat supplied by the boiler for evaporating the weight P. The result thus obtained is not, however, of much use, as the thermal efficiency may be known from a simple calculation, without employing the entropy diagram.

In the entropy cycle $A' B' C' D' E' F'$ (Fig. 29), the curve $A'_{\circ} C'_{\circ}$ being the entropy for water, and X G the curve of saturated steam, the position of the expansion curve D' E' between these two gives the dryness fraction at each point during expansion, and thus shows the important movements of heat. The compression line A' B' also throws some light on this part of the thermal cycle. To understand it, let us study the diagram, Fig. 30, for a weight μ equal to that in the clearance space. Here the horizontal ordinate $a'_{\circ} a'$ is the entropy of this weight of dry saturated steam, $a' b'$ is the compression line, $a'_{\circ} c'_{\circ}$ is the entropy line for the same weight of water. Thus, the portions of horizontals between $a'_{\circ} b'_{\circ}$ and $a' b'$ being the entropy of the steam during compression, are equal to the corresponding horizontal ordinates between $A'_{\circ} B'_{\circ}$ and A' B', Fig. 29. The area $a' b' b_1 a_1$, Fig. 30, represents the heat abstracted by the walls during compression, and may also be found indirectly in Fig. 29.

The line $A'_{\circ} G$ gives the entropy of the weight $P + \mu$ of steam per stroke if dry and saturated, $A'_{\circ} A'$ being for the weight μ and the remainder A' G for the weight P. Thus for the latter we get the curves A' E and F G. The ideal cycle for an engine using P weight of steam per stroke would be A' E F H. Assuming for both the ideal

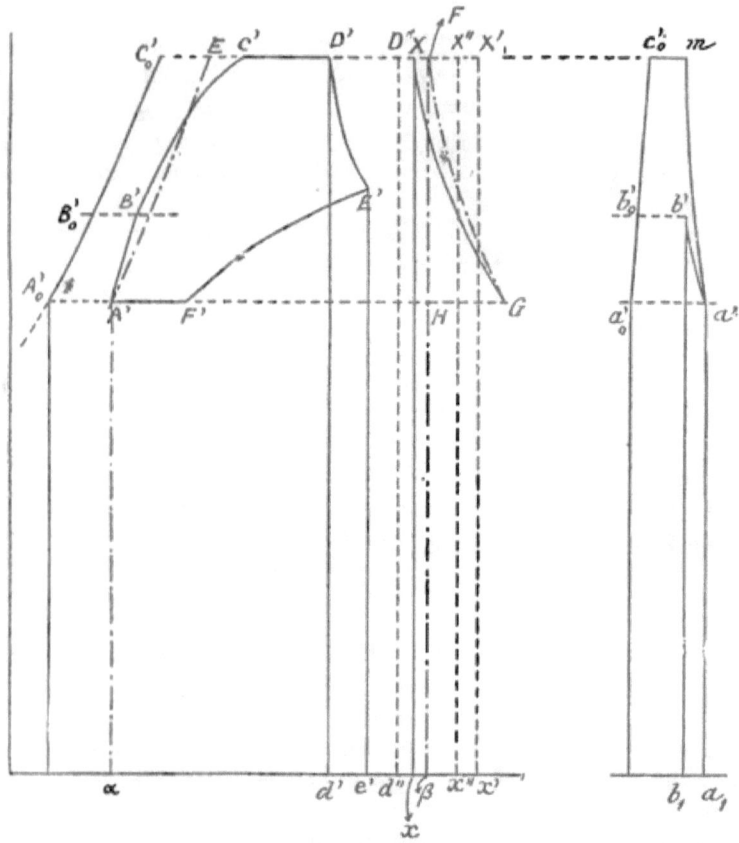

FIGS. 29 AND 30.—ALTERATIONS IN ACTUAL ENTROPY DIAGRAMS.

and the actual engine that the water is pumped into the boiler at the temperature of the condenser, the efficiency of the former will be

$$\frac{A'\,E\,F\,H}{a\,A'\,E\,F\,\beta};$$

while the efficiency of the actual engine for the same expenditure of heat will be

$$\frac{A'\,B'\,C'\,D'\,E'\,F'}{a\,A'\,E\,F\,\beta}.$$

Thus the efficiency of the actual as compared with the ideal engine is

$$\frac{A'\ B'\ C'\ D'\ E'\ F'}{A'\ E\ F\ H}.$$

The difference between **unity** and this last fraction accounts for losses due to imperfect **compression**, wall action, and incomplete expansion. The latter **is, however, an unavoidable defect** if the cylinder volume is limited, as **in most engines. Thus the standard** of efficiency for an ideal engine, **unless corrected for incomplete expansion, may** convey a false impression of the possible perfection attainable.

XXVII. *Wall Action, as shown in Entropy Diagrams.*—We see from the above that the admission of steam into a cylinder is accompanied by condensation. At point C of the indicator diagram, Fig. 28, a weight of steam $\mu + y$ with dryness fraction x_1 fills the clearance, leaving a weight $(\mu + y)(1 - x_1)$ which is present as water on the walls at this moment. This moisture is the result of compression with its accompanying wall action, and of what is supposed to be the instantaneous filling of the clearance volume with boiler steam. At the end of admission, the moisture on the walls corresponds to the missing portion D' X of the entropy diagram, Fig. 29, and the weight of water then present is

$$\frac{D'\ X}{C'_o\ X} \times (P + \mu).$$

Thus the condensation during admission is estimated by subtracting from the total the water present at point *c* or

$$(\mu + y)(1 - x_1),$$

to which corresponds a loss of entropy equal to D'' X. D' D'' is thus the loss of entropy for condensation during admission, and the rectangle D' D'' *d''* *d'* represents the heat absorbed, or the wall action during this period.

If the cylinder is jacketed, a certain quantity of steam is condensed in the jacket, and the heat required to evaporate it must be added to the diagram as heat expended.[*] To compare the heat areas, it may be added on the right of the diagram, Fig. 29, and shown by the rectangle F X' *x'* β. If the quantity of steam condensed by radiation from the external wall of the jacket is known, we can subdivide this area by the vertical X'' *x''*, the area to the right of this line showing the heat lost by radiation.

---

[*] The water from the jacket is supposed to be pumped into the boiler without any loss of temperature, and thus it is not necessary to account for the heat contained in it. If such is not the case, this heat ought to be allowed for.

Having now determined the exchanges of heat during the consecutive phases of the cycle, we may sum them up as follows :

Heat withdrawn from the steam by the internal walls during—	Heat restored to the steam from the internal walls during—
I. Compression : $a' b' b_1 a_1$, Fig. 30.	III. Expansion : $D' E' e' d'$, Fig. 29.
II. Admission : $D'D'' d'' d'$, Fig. 29.	IV. Exhaust : ϕ unknown.

V. Heat communicated by the jacket during a complete cycle, excluding radiation, $F X'' x'' \beta$.

For the complete cycle, the heat given up by the cylinder walls to the steam is in excess of that passing from the steam to the metal, the difference being the heat supplied by the jacket. Thus we have the further equation :

$$III + \phi - (I + II) = V,$$

from whence we calculate ϕ.

Wire-drawing of Steam.—In the foregoing considerations we have neglected the throttling of the steam, and the consequent loss of pressure which takes place during admission and exhaust. The heat actually turned into work may always be known, if the lines of the $p\,v$ diagram are replaced by imaginary reversible operations, forming a closed cycle and giving the same area of work. The heat given up to the condenser (see paragraph XXIV) will not be affected by this substitution, nor will it alter the work done on the fluid. If

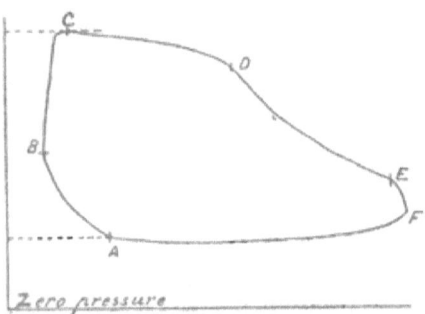

FIG. 31.—ACTUAL INDICATOR DIAGRAM.

wire-drawing takes place to any extent during admission, with incomplete compression, the action of the walls may also be shown separately for this period, as explained hereafter.

Let us next consider the indicator curve A B C D E F (Fig. 31), in which the line A B shows compression to be imperfect, and the admission line C D marks a fall in pressure due to throttling in the steam pipe and ports. At D the admission valve closes, and the exhaust opens at E. We will suppose, as before, that μ is the weight of fluid enclosed in the clearance space, and P the weight of fresh steam coming from the boiler per stroke. If we take the indicator curve as showing the changes of state of the weight $P + \mu$ enclosed in the cylinder, and heated

or cooled externally in such a way as to produce the variations in pressure and volume of Fig. 31, we got the entropy diagram *a b c d e f*,
Fig. 32. Here L and **S** are the entropy curves for **water and** for
saturated steam of the weight P + μ.

As we have already said, if L' be carried out to represent the entropy
of the weight P of water **only,** such intervals as *a' a₂* show the entropy
of the remaining weight **of water μ.** As the interval between L and
a b gives the entropy for **the** vaporised part of the weight μ, it follows
that the abscissæ between **L' and a b** represent **the** total entropy (for
both water and steam) **of the weight μ shut into** the clearance during
compression. Were *a b* parallel to L' compression would be adiabatic.
In Fig. 32 the position **of this line with** reference to L' shows that heat

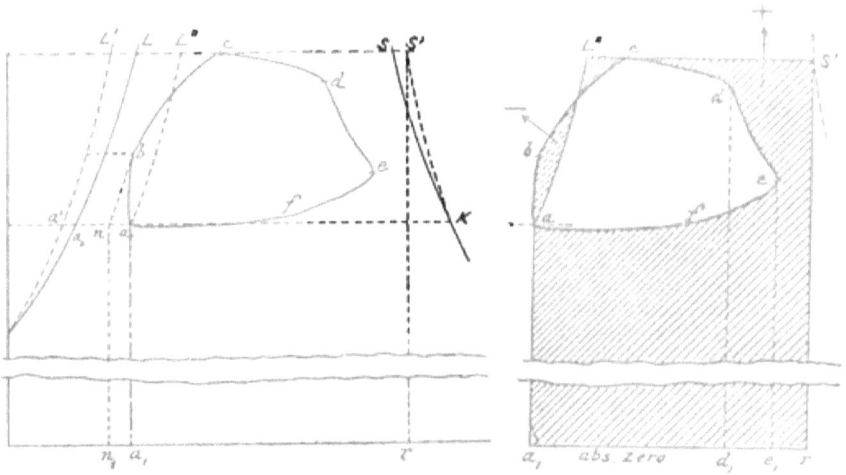

FIGS. **32 AND** 33.—MOVEMENTS OF HEAT.

is given up to the walls, and therefore compression is not adiabatic ; this
heat is represented by **the** area *n₁ n b a a₁*, *n b* being parallel to L'.

The total **heat** supplied to the cycle is that of the weight of steam P
withdrawn **from** the boiler with a dryness fraction assumed to be equal
to unity. **Let us trace the** two curves L'' and S' forming, with the two
temperature ordinates, **the entropy diagram for this weight** P, *a* L'' being
carried out parallel to *a'* L', **because both curves relate** to the same
weight of water. **As** *a* K **is the entropy of the weight** P **of dry
saturated** steam, the saturation **curve S' must naturally pass** through
point K. The heat supplied **to the weight of steam P will be** repre-
sented by the area *a₁* *a* L''S'*r*, the boiler being fed with **water at** the
temperature of point *a*, while the **heat turned into work is** *a b c d e f.*

The difference between these two areas is shown by the shaded surfaces in Fig. 33, the part marked in full lines being positive and the dotted portion negative. This shaded area represents the sum of all the losses of heat shown in the diagram. If M be this area, it must be equal to

1. Heat C given up to the walls during compression.
2. Heat A „ „ admission.
3. Heat of the exhaust steam shown in Fig. 33 by the area $a_1\, a\, e\, e_1$, less
4. Heat refunded per stroke to the steam during expansion, or the area $d_1\, d\, e\, e_1$, which must be subtracted from the above quantities of heat. Thus we get the equation

$$M = C + A + a_1\, a\, e\, e_1 - d_1\, d\, e\, e_1,$$

or

$$C + A = M - a_1\, a\, e\, e_1 + d_1\, d\, e\, e_1.$$

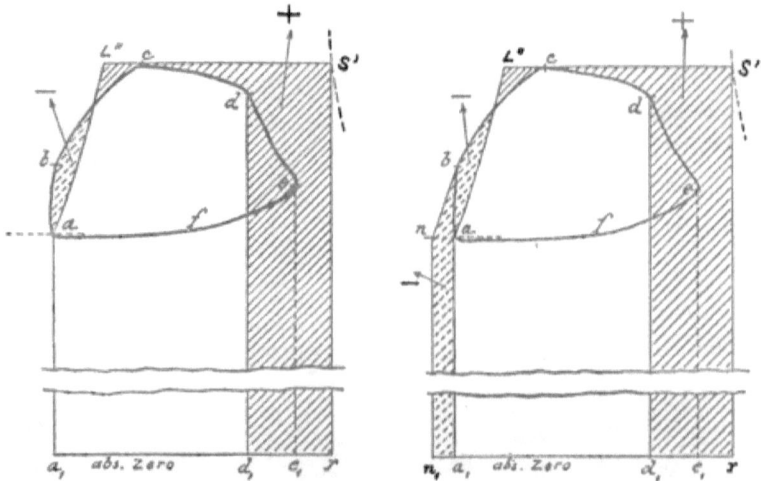

FIGS. 34 AND 35.—MOVEMENTS OF HEAT

The heat absorbed by the walls during compression and admission is thus shown by the shaded areas in Fig. 34, the area marked with dotted lines being subtracted, as we have said. As we know the value of heat C from area $n_1\, n\, b\, a\, a_1$, Fig. 32, we can mark off A, merely by subtracting C from the shaded areas of Fig. 34. This has been done in Fig. 35, in which the heat absorbed by the walls during admission only is shown; all the area marked in dotted lines has to be subtracted.

By means of this graphic method it is not even necessary to find by calculation, as in paragraph XXVI, the weight of steam required to fill the clearance space, nor its dryness fraction. The calculation is useless, and may be dispensed with.

These remarks show that, by means of the entropy diagram, we can analyse quickly and without calculation the utilisation of the heat supplied to an engine per stroke, in the way described by Hirn. As the results are worked out geometrically, nearly all possibility of error is avoided, and the great advantage is also afforded of following continuously the processes of expansion, compression, and their accompanying movements of heat. Finally, we see that by adding or taking away from the diagram a rectangular area of corresponding size, we can allow for and represent the heat lost by radiation, if the cylinder is unjacketed, or that coming from the jacket through the walls, if the cylinder is jacketed and the water from it is measured.

XXVIII. *Application of the above remarks to a Trial of an Actual Engine.*—A single cylinder, non-condensing, horizontal engine, with steam jacket on the barrel only, was selected for this trial. The valve gear consists of two ordinary slide valves, one at each end, worked from one eccentric. The cut-off was obtained by two special slide valves driven partly from the main valves, and partly from an oscillating gear worked by a second eccentric. A vertical wedge actuated and held in position by the governor was so arranged as to give a rapid cut off. The trial lasted about nine hours, but we have chosen a period of four hours, during which the load was practically constant.

From the twelve sets of diagrams taken during this time, we have selected one in which the work approximated most closely to the mean power developed, and treated it according to a method described below.

The data of the trial are—

1. Diameter of piston, 500 millimetres.
2.   „   piston rod (crank side), 93 millimetres.
3.   „   „   (opposite side), 75 millimetres.
4. Duration of the trial, 4 hours 9½ minutes.
5. Revolutions per minute, 56·29.
6. Mean I.H.P.* (crank side), 51·636 .. .. .. } Total I.H.P.
   „   „   (lower side), 49·177 .. .. .. } 100,813.
7. Nearest indicator diagrams (crank side), 51,745 } Total I.H.P.
   „   „   (lower side), 48,324 } 100,069.

---

* The metric I.H.P. is equal to 75 kilogrammetres, the English I.H.P. to 76·041 kilogrammetres; metric I.H.P. = 0·986 English I.H.P.

8. Feed water per I.H.P. per hour.

Admitted to the cylinder, 11·93 kilos.｝   Total,
Condensed in the jacket,   1·01 „ ｝ 12·94 kilos.

The chemical test showed no priming in the steam.

9. Mean weight of steam admitted to the cylinder per stroke, 0·18279 kilo.

10. Condensation in the jacket per stroke, 0·00895 kilo.

11. Working pressure in the boiler, 6·6 atmospheres.

12. Volume of the clearance including the ports, 0·00984 cubic metre.

13. Volume swept by the piston (mean of both sides), 0·190745 cubic metre.

14. Clearance surface exposed to the steam at the beginning of admission (this surface was not jacketed), 1·16 square metre.

15. Ratio of the jacketed to the total internal surface, 62 per cent.

To make use of the diagram selected as nearest the mean, we ought to know the weight of steam admitted during the two corresponding strokes. This weight can be approximately calculated from the mean consumption in proportion to the power developed (lines 6, 7 and 9 of the Table). The condensation in the jacket, which is specially influenced by the fall in temperature, and independent of slight variations in the admission, is taken as constant for each stroke. As the indicator curves differed very slightly on the two sides of the piston, they have been combined in one curve, Fig. 36, for which the weight of steam is

Steam admitted to the cylinder, 0·18144 kilo.
„ condensed in the jacket, 0·00895 „

This indicator curve forms a basis for tracing the thermal diagram, Fig. 37. It is not necessary to know the weight of steam used, to begin with. The entropy scale can be corrected afterwards, and the diagram adapted (as was done with the gas engine diagram, see paragraph XIII) to the weight of working steam here considered.* In the original drawing the scales chosen are

Temperature   1 millimetre per degree C.
Entropy   100   „   unit of entropy.
Pressure   10   „   kilo. per square centimetre.

For the tangents $\frac{d\,p}{d\,\mathrm{T}}$ (see paragraph XIX) the scales for p and T may be arbitrary, but care must be taken to keep the size of the diagram,

* The drawing has been reduced one-half for printing, and the areas therefore are one-quarter the original size.

and therefore the scale of volumes, within reasonable limits. The above scale of temperature was adopted in the original drawing, and the scale of pressures doubled.

All the data required for drawing the main outlines of the diagrams will be found in Table III in the Appendix. It is much better to have this part of the diagram prepared beforehand.

We must next draw the indicator diagram, Fig. 36, to a suitable scale. The volume of the clearance must be marked off on it, and the ordinate $x\,y$ drawn parallel to the line of atmospheric pressure for a given temperature, say 150° C. The length x, 13 is the actual volume occupied at this pressure by the steam admitted to the cylinder, added to the weight of steam compressed into the clearance. The volume of this steam, which at 150° C. is entirely converted into saturated steam, may be calculated and plotted at $x\,y$, y being therefore a point on the saturation curve. To the left of the diagram, Fig. 37, X Y is the same volume as $x\,y$, but to a different scale. To find any point on this diagram, for example point 13, the volumes must be reduced in the following proportion :

$$\frac{X,\,13}{x,\,13} = \frac{X\,Y}{x\,y}.$$

Having thus fixed the position of one point, we have only to apply the same process for all the other points, the abscissæ of the indicator diagram being enlarged in the same proportion, and thus the complete curve is obtained: 1, 2, 3 . . . 8, 9, 10, 11 . . . . 16, 17, 19. The entropy curve can be plotted from it by means of a T-square.

To find the weight of working fluid, note first that the steam admitted from the boiler per stroke weighs P = 0·18144 kilo., to which we must add the weight μ compressed into the clearance; the volume of steam present at exhaust at the temperature of discharge, 101·2° C., and measured from the indicator diagram, is 0·02679 cubic metre. The specific weight of steam at this temperature being 0·63, we have

Weight of steam compressed into the clearance = 0·01688 kilo.

Total weight P + μ during expansion is

$$P + \mu = 0·18144 + 0·01688 = 0·19832 \text{ kilo.}$$

After tracing the diagram the entropy scale must be enlarged in proportion, and multiplied by the ratio of 1 kilo. to the actual weight of steam used. This enlarged scale is drawn below the other in Fig. 37. The scale of volumes must be so chosen that X Y may represent the volume of the weight P + μ, or of 0·19832 kilo. of dry saturated steam at 150° C. Finally, the scale of the heat areas is easily calculated from the temperature and entropy, because each rectangle with a base equal to one unit of entropy, and height equal to 1° C. abs., must represent a calorie.

Discussion of the Diagram.—The compression curve is shown at 1, 2 . . . 5; according to Hirn's hypothesis (paragraph XXV) that the initial cushion steam is saturated, point 1 corresponds to dry saturated steam. To avoid the necessity of tracing a special diagram for studying the compression curve, it will be found convenient to enlarge the volumes to represent the compression of 1 kilo. of steam. This gives the dotted curve Q II III IV V to the left at the bottom for the pv diagram, to the right at the top for the entropy diagram. From the shape of the latter we see that during compression heat is abstracted from the steam by the walls; the dryness fraction of the steam at the end of compression is given by the position of point V. The heat abstracted is represented by the area below Q V in the entropy diagram, multiplied by the actual weight of steam compressed, or μ. The dryness fraction at the end of compression is

$$x_o = 0 \cdot 93.$$

The temperature at this point is 133·2° C. From equations (1) and (2), paragraph XXVI, we get in the present case

$$y = 0 \cdot 0172 \text{ kilo.}$$
$$x_1 = 0 \cdot 98.$$

y is the weight of boiler steam admitted to fill the clearance, x_1 is the dryness fraction of the steam at the end of admission. The heat absorbing action of the walls during admission may all be concentrated into the periods marked 9, 10, 11 on the indicator curve.

According to the diagram the moisture in the steam at point 11 is shown by the entropy line 11 P, but, as we have just seen, part of this moisture was present in the steam at point 9, and therefore before the period 9 to 11 on the pv diagram. This moisture is

$$(\mu + y)(1 - x_1) = 0 \cdot 000682 \text{ kilo.,}$$

and when compared to the total weight of steam $= 0 \cdot 19832$ kilo. will be found to correspond to a diminution of entropy of $P P_o$, which may be neglected. The remainder, 11, P_o, represents the actual condensation produced by wall action during admission.

Heat Efficiency.—To estimate the efficiency of the cycle, the heat turned into work must be compared with the total expenditure of heat. As the weight of boiler steam is P and not $P + \mu$, for which we have the entropy diagram M N P Q, therefore for this weight of steam, P, we must draw to the same scale the area M′ N′ P′ Q shown in dotted lines. To this we add the portion P′ R representing heat absorbed by jacket condensation 0·00895 kilo., which extends downwards to absolute zero. The heat in the water leaving the jacket is not taken into account, because this water may be pumped back into the boiler, and the heat in it thus utilised.

Results shown by the Diagram :—

1. Dryness fraction at cut-off (point 11), 0·595.

2. Dryness fraction at the opening of exhaust (point 17), 0·745.

3. Heat turned into indicated work (closed cycle), 9·27 calories.

4. Heat expended, including the jacket, the condensation water being returned to the boiler, and the feed heated by the exhaust to its own temperature :

> Heat in the cylinder, 100·60 calories⎫ Total 105 calories.
> Heat in the jacket, 4·40 calories⎭

5. Thermal efficiency of the actual engine, or ratio of numbers 3 to 4, 8·83 per cent.

6. Thermal efficiency of the ideal engine having no clearance, no wall action, and complete adiabatic expansion, 13·29 per cent. (This efficiency is the ratio of the area M N P S to the area M N P down to absolute zero. In calculating it, the actual weight of fluid employed in the cycle is of no consequence.)

7. Efficiency of the actual as compared with the ideal engine, or ratio of results 5 and 6 = 66 per cent.

8. Losses of heat from wall action, radiation, and incomplete compression and expansion = 34 per cent.

Effect of the Walls.—The heat lost by radiation not having been measured, must next be calculated from the extent of the surfaces exposed to radiation, which are in round numbers 6 square metres, and their partial protection by polished wrought-iron plates. Thus the mean loss by radiation per stroke may be taken at 1·15 calorie.

9. Continuing our enumeration of results, we may thus reckon : Heat radiated externally from the jacket, walls of the steam chest, and unprotected steam pipes = 1·15 calorie.

10. Total heat supplied by the jacket (see line 4) = 4·4 calories.

11. Difference between lines 9 and 10, representing the heat communicated by the jacket to the steam in the cylinder per stroke, through the walls, = 3·25 calories.

12. Heat absorbed by the walls during compression, measured from below the line Q V of the entropy diagram, Fig. 37 = 1·10 calorie.

13. Heat absorbed by the walls during the opening of the admission valve = 39·61 calories.

14. Heat refunded by the walls to the steam during expansion, or area defined by the expansion curve, 11, 12 . . . 17, Fig. 37 = 22·49 calories.

15. Heat refunded by the walls to the steam during exhaust, or ϕ from the equation $\phi + 14 = 11 + 12 + 13$; $\phi = 21·47$ calories.

16. Heat lost to the exhaust, or area defined by the line 17, 19, 1 = 73·50 calories.

17. Balance showing the distribution of the heat *per stroke*.

	Calories			Calories
Heat expended (line 4):		Heat turned into work		
In the cylinder . .	100·60	(line 3)		9·27
In the jacket . . .	4·40	Heat lost by radiation		
		(line 9)		1·15
		Heat lost by the walls to		
		the exhaust (line 15) .		21·47
		Heat of the exhaust steam		
		(line 16)		73·50
Total calories	105·00	Total calories		105·39

The totals of the two columns should agree, but their accuracy depends on the correctness of the drawings and planimetric measurements. The error, with care, will not attain 0·4 per cent., and may be neglected.

The heat shown under head 15 requires a word of explanation. It is generally called "*waste of heat to exhaust*," but this expression conveys the false notion, that in an ideal engine these 21·47 calories could be turned into work. Of course, if there were no wall action this waste would not exist, but the loss of heat in the exhaust steam would be much higher, because of the greater dryness of the steam, and therefore the waste shown at line 16 would be increased.

This example will sufficiently explain the application of the entropy diagram to a steam engine trial. The only data required for it are the mean I.H.P. from the indicator diagrams, exact dimensions of the cylinder and clearance, consumption of steam per stroke in the cylinder and jacket, and radiation per stroke. In the above analysis the valves and piston are supposed to be perfectly steam-tight. If this were not the case the conclusions arrived at would be inaccurate, because all the steam shown in the indicator diagram as missing, would be reckoned as condensed by the action of the walls, whereas part of the waste would be due to leakage. This loss by leakage is especially important during the period of compression, when the effect of leaks upon the small mass of compressed steam may be very considerable. The compression curve will show a great loss of heat, erroneously attributed to the rapid cooling action of the walls.

The study of a compound expansion engine is complicated by the variation in the weight of steam passing through the successive cylinders, particularly if the jackets are supplied with working steam. The loss of heat in the water **from** each jacket must be deducted, in order to estimate the weight of **steam** admitted per stroke. Another difficulty arises from the fact that the period of admission in each cylinder does not coincide with the exhaust from the preceding cylinder. For strict accuracy the cycle of the receiver should be added to the entropy diagram, unless the dimensions of the receiver are very large, as in most land engines.[*]

XXIX. *Remarks on Steam Turbines.*—In hydraulic turbines the power generated is transferred to the wheel as kinetic energy, and only a small portion of it is communicated to the tail water. Steam turbines are based on the same principle. Thus in the Parsons high-speed turbine, a series of axial wheels or vanes on the same shaft are separated by an equal number of rings with fixed vanes. The head of pressure between the outflow of one wheel and the inflow of the next is utilised to impart speed to the steam, the vanes serving to direct and regulate this energy. If the conditions of maximum efficiency are carefully complied with, the mix-

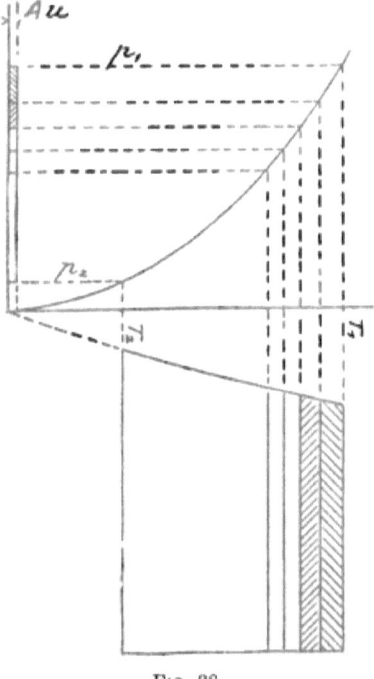

Fig. 38.

ture of steam and water issuing from the last wheel would practically have parted with all its energy. As the steam passes through each wheel its energy of motion is converted into work done on the shaft, without change of pressure. If the friction, which may be considerable, be neglected, we may represent the quantity of heat transformed into energy, and distributed through the successive vanes of the turbine,

---

[*] See 'Engineering,' vol. lvi. January 3, 1896, where an example by the Author of an entropy diagram for a compound engine is given.

by a series of bands or shaded areas, Fig. 38. The sum of the smaller areas A $(p_1 - p_2)$ u represents the heat equivalent to the work of feeding the boiler. The larger areas to the right show the net heat turned into actual work, and are the same as for a steam engine of the ordinary type. Thus the ideal turbine would utilise the same quantity of heat within the same limits of temperature as the ideal steam engine. The losses of heat in the two types of motor are quite distinct, as there is practically no wall action in steam turbines, but other causes of waste exist, such as loss of heat by friction, and dissipation of heat in various ways.

APPENDIX

TABLE I.—FOR CALCULATING q (HEAT OF THE LIQUID). (*See Paragraph* XV).

Name of Liquid.	a.	b.	c.	Reference.
Water	1	0·00002	0·0000003	* Ledoux.
Ether	0·52901	0·0002959	..	† Zeuner.
Sulfurous acid . .	0·36333 *	0·000004	..	
Ammonia . . . . {	1·0058 *	0·001829	..	
{	1·01235 †	0·004189	..	

TABLE II.—HEAT OF EVAPORATION. (*See Paragraph* XV).

Name of Liquid.	A.	B.	C.	D.	Reference.
Water	606·5	− 0·635	− 0·00002	−0·0000003	* Ledoux.
Ether	94	− 0·07901	− 0·0008514	..	† Zeuner.
Sulfurous acid . .	91·396 *	− 0·2361	− 0·000135	..	
Ammonia . . . {	313·63 *	− 0·6250	− 0·002111	..	
{	314·865 †	− 0·64303	− 0·004714	..	

TABLE III.—PROPERTIES OF STEAM.

t, Temp. C.	T, Abs. Temp.	$\frac{p}{10,000}$.	$\frac{dp}{dt}$.	q, Heat of the Liquid. Calories.	Entropy of the Liquid.	r, Heat of Evaporation. Calories.	$\frac{r}{T}$. Heat of Evaporation ÷ Absolute Temperature	γ. †
0	273	0·0063	..	0 00	0·000	606·50	..	0·005
10	283	0·0125	..	10·00	0·036	599·55	..	0·009
20	293	0·0236	..	20·01	0·071	592·59	..	0·017
30	303	0·0429	..	30·03	0·104	585·62	..	0·030
40	313	0·0747	..	40·05	0·137	578·64	1·84878	0·051
50	323	0·1251	..	50·09	0·169	571·66	..	0·083
60	333	0·2023	93·97	60·14	0·199	564·66	1·69567	0·131
70	343	0·3169	137·51	70·20	0·229	557·65	..	0·199
80	353	0·4822	195·76	80·28	0·258	550·62	1·5599	0·296
90	363	0·7144	272·00	90·38	0·286	543·57	..	0·428
100	373	1·0334	369·78	100·50	0·314	536·50	1·43836	0·606
110	383	1·4623	492·48	110·64	0·341	529·41	..	0·839
120	393	2·0278	644·93	120·81	0·367	522·29	1·32873	1·141
130	403	2·7607	827·87	131·00	0·392	515·15	..	1·524
140	413	3·6953	1048·02	141·21	0·417	507·99	1·22987	2·004
150	423	4·8695	1307·93	151·46	0·442	500·79	..	2·597
160	433	6·3250	1610·99	161·74	0·466	493·56	1·14012	3·320
170	443	8·1063	1960·28	172·05	0·490	486·30	..	4·192
180	453	10·2611	2363·55	182·40	0·513	479·00	1·05739	5·230
190	463	12·8396	2808·10	192·78	0·535	471·67	..	6·456
200	473	15·8939	3310·76	203·20	0·558	464·30	0·98160	7·888

* p is in kilogrammes per sq. metre.   † Weight in kilogrammes of a cubic metre of steam.

TABLE IV.—ENTROPY OF CARBONIC ACID (REGNAULT AND ZEUNER).*

t, Temp. C.	T, Abs. Temp.	$\frac{p}{10,000}$	$\frac{dp}{dt}$	q, Heat of the Liquid.	Entropy of the Liquid.	r, Heat of Evaporation.	$\frac{r}{T}$. Heat of Evaporation. Absolute Temperature	γ.
− 30	243	15·1441	4724·1	− 15·88	− 0·0612	69·10	0·2844	37·76
− 25	248	17·6844	5435·1	− 14·34	− 0·0549	68·23	0·2751	44·40
− 20	253	20·5877	6240·2	− 12·36	− 0·0469	66·85	0·2642	52·25
− 10	263	27·6546	7958·6	− 7·07	− 0·0264	62·58	0·2379	72·52
0	273	36·5823	9937·5	0·00	0	56·28	0·2061	100·60
10	283	47·4749	12096·1	8·85	0·0318	47·94	0·1694	138·70
20	293	60·7846	11361·3	19·47	0·0686	37·58	0·1283	191·57
30	303	76·3065	16648·8	..	..	..	..	..

* The entropy of the liquid and of steam differ slightly from the figures given **by** M. Schröter, which have been used for drawing the diagram, Fig. 21.

TABLE V.—ENTROPY OF AMMONIA.

t, Temperature C.	Entropy of the Liquid.	$\frac{r}{T}$. Heat of Evaporation. Absolute Temperature	$\frac{p}{10,000}$.
− 40	− 0·1331	1·4293	0·7187
− 30	− 0·1029	1·3576	1·1890
− 20	− 0·0706	1·2849	1·9004
− 10	− 0·0362	1·2198	2·9227
0	0·0000	1·1533	4·3475
10	0·0379	1·0882	6·2710
20	0·0774	1·0243	8·7293
30	0·1184	0·9615	12·0089
40	0·1608	0·8997	16·0107

TABLE VI.—ENTROPY OF SULFUROUS ACID (ZEUNER AND LEDOUX).

t, Temperature C.	ZEUNER.		LEDOUX.	
	Entropy of the Liquid.	$\frac{r}{T}$. Heat of Evaporation. Absolute Temperature	Entropy of the Liquid.	$\frac{r}{T}$. Heat of Evaporation. Absolute Temperature
− 40	− 0·0386	0·4124	..	..
− 30	− 0·0323	0·3946	− 0·0122	0·4046
− 20	− 0·0236	0·3755	− 0·0276	0·3796
− 10	− 0·0128	0·3553	− 0·0135	0·3564
0	0·0000	0·3341	0·0030	0·3245
10	0·0147	0·3120	0·0131	0·3145
20	0·0310	0·2891	0·0257	0·2956
30	0·0490	0·2655	0·0380	0·2778
40	0·0684	0·2412	0·0499	0·2610

NOTES FOR CONVERTING METRIC TO ENGLISH UNITS.

Temperatures.

Centigrade Scale.		Fahrenheit Scale.
0°	=	32°
100°	=	212°

For converting Centigrade degrees to Fahrenheit, multiply the temperatures Centigrade by 1·8 and add 32 to the result.

Inversely, for converting Fahrenheit degrees into Centigrade, subtract the constant 32 and divide the rest by 1·8.

Heat Units.

1 calorie = 3·968 B.T.U.
1 B.T.U. = 0·252 calorie.
Specific heats are alike in metric or English units.

Lengths.

1 metre = 3·2809 English feet.
1 English foot = 0·304794 metre.
1 inch = 0·0253995 metre.

Areas.

1 square metre = 10·7642 square feet.
1 square foot = 0·09290 square metre.
1 square inch = 0·00064513 square metre.

Volumes.

1 cubic metre = 35·3161 cubic feet.
1 cubic foot = 0·028315 cubic metre.
1 cubic inch = 0·000016386 cubic metre.

Weights.

1 kilogramme = 2·2046 pounds.
1 pound = 0·4536 kilogramme.

Pressures.

1 atmosphere = 760 millimetres of mercury = 14·696 pounds per square inch.
1 kilogramme per square centimetre = 14·223 pounds per square inch.
1 pound per square inch = 0·0703 kilogramme per square centimetre.

Work, Power.

75 kilogrammetres = 542·47 foot-pounds.
75 kilogrammetres per second = 1 metric horse-power = 542·47 foot-pounds per second.
550 foot-pounds per second = 1 English horse-power = 76·041 kilogrammetres per second.

LONDON: PRINTED BY WILLIAM CLOWES AND SONS, LIMITED, STAMFORD STREET AND CHARING CROSS.

www.ingramcontent.com/pod-product-compliance
Lightning Source LLC
Chambersburg PA
CBHW032350020726
47499CB00008B/2689

* 9 7 8 3 3 3 7 4 0 6 2 3 3 *